Fear the Beast Within

Book One: The Fear Series

Authored By:
L R Barrett-Durham
and E G Glover

Illustrated By:
L R Barrett-Durham

Dedication by
L R Barrett-Durham

In loving memory of my matchless
grandmother, Mildred Barrett,
who is responsible for every
creative bone in my body.

Dedication by
E G Glover

In loving memory of my son,
William James Glover,
whom I never knew in this world,
but will in the next.

**Books by
L R Barrett-Durham
and E G Glover**

<u>The Fear Series</u>:
Fear the Beast Within
Fear the Thirst Within
(Winter 2012)

**Books by
L R Barrett-Durham**

<u>The Trust Series</u>:
Never Trust a Sorcerer
Always Trust Your Honor

Fear of the unknown,

The strength to withstand.

Beast rears the evil alone,

Within you, it's power outmanned.

- E G Glover

Prologue

Wallachia · 1742

The lyrical music of the Roma camp did little to appease Yeaserna as she watched the love of her life marry another woman.

The camp's center was overflowing with visitors from the bride's village nearby, as well as members of their own nomadic tribe.

The bonfires blazing in the center of the circle of wagons matched the rage burning within her.

He belongs to me!

Dak had been a part of her soul for their entire lives, and now he had agreed to an arranged marriage to a lowly peasant from the village a few miles away and planned to leave the Roma and their wandering ways for good.

Sondra isn't even pleasing to the eyes!

But there the harlot stood, next to Dak in front of the fire, her hair bound up with pins so that her red tresses flowed down her back like a waterfall of fire.

Her palms itched with the need to strangle the girl for taking away her hopes and dreams.

On an impulse she didn't understand, she began a slow ancient chant that quickly turned into something monstrous and seething.

When she finished, she was on the ground on her knees.

Her kin stood next to her, looking at her glowing eyes in horror.

She heard Dak cry out and watched her heart's plea come to life.

Dak grabbed his chest at the same instant Yeaserna grabbed her own, and the smell of burning skin wafted through the air.

Sondra ran to Dak in concern, and he held her a moment before stepping back and doubling over in pain.

Dak's face began to elongate, and his piercing cry became guttural as his body transformed into a wolf-like beast.

Sondra watched in horror, stepping back and making a gesture to fend off the evil eye.

The Roma people and the villagers screamed and ran toward the wagons as the beast sent forth a horrendous howl.

Sondra spoke to the beast in a soothing tone, but Dak only snarled back at her, the feral gleam in his canine eyes burning brightly in the firelight.

The bride stepped back farther and glanced at Yeaserna for just a moment before an unworldly and sinister sensation drove her hand to the dagger underneath her clothing.

Sondra's arm struggled against a force not her own, and her eyes filled with fear as she unwillingly plunged the dagger into her own heart.

Sondra fell near the fire, blood dripping from her rosy lips, the bloody blade still gripped in her hand.

Yeaserna walked backward, a sense of satisfaction overwhelming her.

As soon as Sondra had drawn her last breath, Dak's transformation reversed, his body contorting back into shape in a white-hot blaze of pain.

He stood naked before his dead wife, an angry red welt searing the smooth skin over his aching heart.

His howl of anguish was music to Yeaserna's ears.

Chapter One

Parker's Ridge, TN – 1993

Licah Daciana walked into the school gym. The musty scent of sweat, pimple cream, and cheap cologne overwhelmed her nose. The dim lighting and cheap decorations did nothing to hide the fact that it was still just a gym.

"Why am I here?" she asked herself, shaking her head with the ridiculousness of it.

She turned to walk back out and ran right into a guy half a foot taller than she.

She'd seen him before.

He was a few years older, probably a senior to her freshman.

His red hair was slightly disheveled, but fashionably so, and his brilliant gray eyes glanced over her before he walked past to join up with a few friends.

The hair stood on her arms as he brushed against her and the scar on her chest tingled, but she dismissed the event as static from the cool rush of air coming through the open door.

After shaking her head at the absurd thoughts running through it, she turned back to the room.

She wandered around for a few minutes and then walked over to the refreshment table.

She was reaching for a glass of punch when she felt the oddest tingle race down her spine, and a blazing sensation from the mark over her heart.

She turned and glanced around the room.

She saw the same guy she had just collided with race to the bathroom, knocking students aside as he ran.

Saxton Lyall stood in the gym bathroom, sweat pouring from his fair-skinned brow.

He looked down at his hands, tightly gripping the dirt-smeared sink. They glistened with large droplets and he could see his shaken image in their reflection.

"Not again...not here!!" His breath was raspy and uncontrolled as the words raced from his lips, which felt as though they had been set afire.

Saliva fell from his mouth, landing in the sink below his face.

He dared not look in the mirror.

He knew what he would find behind his burning lips. He had seen the sharply pointed teeth once before.

His feet slipped on the muck-covered floor and he grabbed the sink tighter until he could feel the porcelain begin to give way under his steel grip.

He loosened his hold and stood erect. He instinctively threw his hand over his heart covering the oddly shaped welt that had appeared there not two weeks before.

His heartbeat was more deafening than the music that was currently blasting away outside the locked restroom door.

The school dance had been his friend's idea. He'd really had no desire to be there, especially by himself.

Now it was happening, again.

He had felt this mind-numbing burn once before at the local coffee shop, but it had been much more intense then.

Saxton finally looked into the mirror.

Through the spit-stained glass, his eerie reflection stared back with gray, bloodshot eyes and distended cheeks.

His red hair seemed almost bristled, standing on end like that of an angry animal.

As he gazed deeper into the mirror, he finally opened his mouth, expecting to find elongated.

There was nothing there.

After a few deep breaths, he felt that his heart had slowed to a normal pace.

As he reached for a towel to wipe his forehead, his hands were no longer drowning in sweat.

It had stopped.

Van Pelt High School's Sadie Hawkins dance wasn't exactly bumping, or jumping, for that matter.

Students crowded around the edge of the room, daring each other to take a step toward the center, where condemnation was sure to reign down upon them.

Licah Daciana thought it was asinine.

She hadn't asked anyone to the dance. She hadn't been willing to see the revolt on a boy's face as she stumbled out onto that proverbial limb.

She was an outcast.

Her waist-length black tresses were tied back with a colorful scarf her mother had woven into it before she had left home.

Her gypsy skirt fluttered around her ankles as she walked around the perimeter of the room.

She found a quiet corner and stood with the other onlookers, watching the three young couples who had braved the dance floor.

She raised her glass to them in salute.

Coming from a Romanian family and trying to fit in at a high school in Parker's Ridge, Tennessee was about as hopeless a cause as the young man walking out of the bathroom.

His red hair was wet, and his white Bob Marley t-shirt clung to his chest.

She couldn't remember his name.

He seemed to be out of breath and disoriented.

She ignored the odd sensations inside her and wandered over to where he was leaning against the stacked bleachers.

"Are you okay?" she asked, placing a hand on his shoulder.

His cool gray eyes met hers, and the tingle that had only been slightly on the radar intensified to the point where she gasped aloud and dropped her glass of punch.

His first reaction had been to reach down to pick up the fallen glass, but it was as if a thousand images pierced his mind all at once.

He doubled over, the gaze of this unfamiliar girl broken, but not before the color of her emerald-green eyes were permanently etched into his memory.

"Please, I'm just feeling really sick. I need to go home," he managed to choke out.

She looked down at him, her hand still resting lightly on his shoulder, "You're looking very ill. I don't think you should drive home like…"

As he felt his spine begin to contort, he shot up from his crouched position, pushing away her resting hand, and pleaded, "I'll be fine! I just need to go outside."

He darted away from her without another word, limping as he ran. He could feel the eyes of a hundred people upon him, and the urge to flee was overwhelming.

He could feel the gaze of the beautiful stranger following his movements as he hurried away from her soft touch.

Desperate to escape, he collided with the double gym doors with such force that they nearly knocked him to the ground when they slammed shut behind him.

He staggered into the parking lot, trying to find his old, rusty, brown Camaro.

Before he could begin to get his bearings, a voice came from his right, "Sax! Where the hell are you going?"

Saxton spun to the right and refocused his eyes to see Jackson Milser standing there with an annoyed expression and a fist on one hip.

"Jack, I gotta go home. Something is seriously wrong."

"Damn man, how much of that punch did you drink? I told you not to get too heavy on it. I doctored it up pretty good," he said, removing his planted hand and walking quickly over to Saxton.

"No, it's not the punch, it's..." the endless images poured into his mind again, all being punctuated by the pair of emerald disks he had seen in the eyes of the young girl just moments ago.

"You need me to drive you home? I got Dad's 'vette tonight."

12

Saxton tried not to laugh, knowing that Jackson had a Chevette, not a Corvette. "No, I just need to get to my car."

Jackson stopped and pointed into the dimly lit parking lot, "It's right over there. Exactly where you put it like ten minutes ago."

Saxton hobbled over to his car, quickly opened the door and half sat, half fell into the seat.

Jackson walked up to him and rested his hands on top of the door, "You sure you're gonna be able to drive? You look just like that time you got into Carlos' hunch punch."

Saxton slammed the door shut, almost causing Jackson to lose an arm, "I'm fine. I just need to get outta here!"

Panicking, he started his car and spun out of the parking lot, pelting Jackson with gravel.

"Dude," Jackson yelled at the escaping car, "I was just trying to get you outta the house and have a good time for once in your life. Geez!"

Licah stared at the door where the hysterical guy had escaped.

She now remembered where she had seen him before. He had done the same thing to her at McGuire's.

She had been sitting with Jessica, having a cup of coffee, when he had approached their table as if he were about to start a conversation.

As soon as their eyes had met, Licah had felt a burning pain over her heart.

Shortly thereafter, he'd fled the coffee shop, and she hadn't seen him again until tonight.

She looked around the room and noticed that their scene had attracted quite a bit of attention.

Great. Now they would think her even more of a freak.

She picked up the fallen glass, not bothering to wipe up the spill, and set it on the table closest to the door.

As she was leaving, a senior named Jack, your typical jock type, stomped past her as if he were really pissed off.

She was so sick of this little Podunk town. Why couldn't they just go back to New York?

She climbed into her Nissan truck and rolled down the windows.

The air was chilly, but the tingling sensation on her burn combined with the embarrassment of the scene with the guy had her needing it.

She turned up the radio and listened to Trent Reznor.

Head like a hole, black as your soul, I'd rather die, than give you control.

She felt there couldn't be a more perfectly wretched song for a more perfectly wretched evening.

Saxton could feel the cool mid-November breeze gusting through the window as he sped away from Van Pelt High.

He was so shaken by the events in the gym that he feared to even look in his rearview mirror.

The flood of images that came over him was so intense and overwhelming that he could hardly remember any details of what he had seen.

The only constant within his mind were the eyes of the girl that had tried to comfort him at the dance.

He didn't even know her name.

He assumed she must be the girl of the Romanian family that had moved into the area some time ago, but he had never actually spoken to her or even seen her until about a week ago, or was it two?

He looked down at his white shirt; the Marley design was covered in drying sweat and moist gravel dust.

He knew he was going to hear it from Jackson the following Monday at school for ditching the dance so early.

The only reason he had even darkened the door of the gym was to appease his nagging friend.

His looked down at the car's dash gauges.

He knew he had been low on gas when he had arrived at the school, but he hadn't realized he had been that low.

He noted his speed and quickly pressed the brake.

"Ninety miles per hour," he muttered to himself.

Then it dawned on him as he glanced at the dashboard clock; he had been driving for nearly an hour.

His trip home should have been, at worst, fifteen minutes.

He brought the old Camaro to a screeching halt on the side of the road and cut the engine.

He had been driving in circles.

He stared out the driver's side window, and all he saw were trees and the occasional aluminum can marking the roadside.

The sounds of crickets and frogs filled his ears, and the cool air burned the inside of his nostrils.

"I must be losing my mind!" he said out loud with a little more force than he'd meant to.

Letting out a troubled sigh, he started the car back up and headed toward home.

He fiddled with the radio knob and came across a familiar song. He turned up the volume.

Where had he recently heard that song?

McGuire's Brewhouse! That song, that girl!

His vision glazed as he drove down the familiar country road, remembering the horror he had experienced not so long ago at McGuire's.

Saxton sat at one of the many small tables littered about the coffee shop waiting on Jackson to meet him, so they could make plans for the upcoming dance.

He hated dances, or at least he hated the awkwardness of talking to a girl. He had never liked approaching women when it came to dating. It was just easier for him to lurk in the shadows and not be noticed.

The only reason Jackson had been able to convince him to go at all was the fact that it was a Sadie Hawkins dance. He hadn't had to bother with asking anyone. If anything, the tradition took most of the pressure off of his sheepish demeanor.

While he was waiting for Jackson, he enjoyed the best cup of coffee in town. He watched the steam billow from his coffee cup and placed his nose over the dark brew and deeply inhaled its rich aroma.

"Ah, heaven," he thought.

He looked around the shop at the other tables. There were four other customers scattered about the otherwise empty business, aside from Carlos, the best espresso maker in the universe.

Carlos was only three years older than Saxton and already had his own business. It was funny to most of the youth in town, since Carlos had been voted Class of 1991 Most Likely To Be Found Dead, Face First In a Gutter.

Saxton looked in Carlos' direction and nodded as he took a short swig of his coffee, "Perfect as always, Carlos."

Carlos just rolled his eyes as he wiped down the already clean counter, "Sax, it's just coffee! You'd think I put gold slivers in it by the way you suck that stuff down."

Saxton just smiled. Carlos knew that his shop had the best coffee in the county. It was a tad overpriced, but definitely the best.

"Carlos, have you seen Jackson today? He was supposed to meet me here."

Carlos frowned, "No, I haven't seen Jack. Not that I have been looking."

Smirking at the memory of Carlos and Jackson's last fight, he asked, "Are you still mad at him for losing that bet on the UT game?"

"I'm telling you man, those refs were paid off!"

Carlos stopped scrubbing the counter and went back into the back to find something else to clean.

Not that it needed it.

There wasn't a place in the whole building that Saxton wouldn't be afraid to take a dare and run his bare tongue over.

Saxton's attention was drawn to the door as one of the other customers opened it, and the small, bronze bell over the door chimed.

As one customer exited, another entered.

A girl he had never seen before.

She'd walked up to one of the other customers already sitting in the shop, Jessica Danley.

He only recognized Jessica because of the ever-present purple streak in the back of her hair.

He really didn't know her. All he really knew was that she was a freshman at Van Pelt High.

She was a bit of an oddball, but then again, so was he.

He had talked to her a couple times about music, but other than that, she was almost as unknown to him as the dark haired girl that had entered the shop.

Saxton occasionally glanced in their general direction as he sipped on his coffee.

Carlos returned to his counter at the sound of the door chime and noticed Saxton passively gawking at the two girls' table.

Carlos grinned and snorted at Saxton to gain his attention.

When Saxton saw Carlos smirking at him, he straightened in his chair, and pretended to look at the Halloween decorations that were festively placed here and there.

Actually the decorations were the problem. He couldn't see the new girl because of the flashy-orange pumpkin man hanging in his way.

He finally downed the rest of his coffee, took a deep breath, and started walking over to their table.

He took a long look at the new girl, noticing her long ebony hair and European features.

She was absolutely beautiful.

Their eyes met for a moment and he took another steadying breath and was only a few feet away from her when he felt a sharp burning sensation over his heart.

He stopped in the middle of the shop and waited for it to pass, knowing he had to look like a fool.

The girl looked up at him and rubbed her hand over her chest in the same spot where he was hurting.

After a sudden sharp stomach pain, he turned around and walked to the bathroom, the blush creeping up his neck registering how he must appear to her.

As he reached for the knob he noticed his fingernails were longer than he had ever seen them. And when had his hands gotten so hairy?

He went into the loo and locked the door behind him.

He ran cool water from the tap and gathered some in his palms.

As he reached to splash the water onto his face, he felt his nose long before he should have.

He glanced up in the mirror in surprise and nearly cried out at what he saw.

His red hair had grown shaggy and his nose had lengthened and darkened on the end.

His eyebrows had also grown and the flesh beneath them seemed to have thickened, giving him an animalistic appearance.

His normally full lips had thinned and he opened his mouth to see that his teeth had lengthened and sharpened to points.

His heart jackhammered in his chest and he turned around in circles in the bathroom, which suddenly smelled much more unpleasant than he remembered from moments before.

He wondered what he was going to do.

He was turning into some kind of freak!

He remembered the access door to the loading dock just down the hall from the bathroom.

He cautiously pushed opened the door to ensure sure that no one was in the small hallway, first by looking left and then to the right. All he was able to make out was Carlos busying himself stocking more supplies.

He made a beeline for the door and escaped into the night.

Details after that had gotten fuzzy, other than an insane amount of dodging and jumping as he had fled from McGuire's.

The last coherent memory Saxton had was waking up naked the next morning in some bushes next to his house.

Saxton's vision cleared as he pulled into his driveway, the headlights illuminating the same bushes from that night.

It was an evening he had hoped he could forget, but it appeared that was becoming easier said than done.

Licah opened the door to the small apartment she shared with her mother and was met with a rush of patchouli scent.

Her mother always burned incense.

It was her way of "guarding against demons".

"Maman, I am home," she said, dropping her bag next to the couch.

She wandered past her mother's room and noticed the older woman asleep in a chair, her knitting needles still clutched in her hands.

Licah shook her head and carefully dislodged the yarn, needles, and long scarf her mother had been working with.

After placing them on the table next to the chair, she retrieved an afghan from the bed, also her mother's handy work, and covered her up.

Her mother had insisted they leave New York two years ago because she had said she was getting older and needed a break from the hustle and bustle.

Licah noticed the gray streaks in her mother's black hair and grimaced.

Maybe she was right, but Licah hated it in Parker's Ridge.

At least she'd had friends in New York, where eccentricities were the norm, not the exception.

She walked to her bedroom and took a camisole and a pair of boxers out of her chest of drawers.

She stood in front of her mirror and removed her lacy white poet shirt.

Right above her left breast, there was an angry scar in the shape of an odd circle with five smaller circles above it, topped with what appeared to be scratches.

She still had no clue why it was there.

She had noticed it after leaving the coffee shop that day. It had shown up right after that boy had freaked out on her the first time.

She shrugged and removed her colorful gypsy skirt and put on her shorts and cami.

Boys were weird.

Saxton struggled with his keys, trying to open the front door to his house.

He could see the light was still on in the living room.

His mom was still up.

She hadn't slept much since his dad had passed away.

Saxton's dad had died in an accident at work three years before.

He had worked as a production manager in a metal factory. He had been about to go on his lunch break and had stepped right in front of a forklift carrying tons of metal sheeting and the driver hadn't seen him.

His mom still missed him terribly.

She compensated for her loneliness by reading about the lives of others in the countless romance novels she had collected over the years.

Saxton could not relate to his mom's emotions. As long as he could remember, his dad had worked constantly, often taking trips out of town for work, and was rarely home.

Occasionally, when his dad had been home, he and his mom would tell stories about their youthful days.

His mom had monopolized the sessions with her tales of simpler life in Parker's Ridge.

All he could recall about his dad was that he had deep family roots going back to the Irish of another time, long forgotten.

After the accident in nineteen-ninety, his mom had been anxious to move from the hustle and bustle of Birmingham, Alabama, back to Parker's Ridge, back to old friends and easier times.

She was from the sleepy, little town. He wasn't.

His mom did her best to make him happy there, and it did feel like home.

Most of the time.

After dropping his keys two or three times, he was startled by the front door opening and revealing her.

"Saxton, why are you home so early? I thought you were going to the dance?"

His mother's long auburn hair was pulled up in a ponytail and brushed his aching chest as he walked by her.

"I'm fine mom. Just really wasn't my scene, you know?"

He flopped down on the couch and looked at his mother's chair, a dog-eared book lying on the arm.

"You reading another one of your smut books again?"

She closed the door and returned to her seat. She rolled her eyes and impishly smiled, ignoring his remark.

"Were there not any pretty girls there just dying to dance with you?"

Saxton wanted to lash out at the remark, but thought better of it.

He wanted to tell her of the events that had happened at the dance, but knew it would just worry her, and she already worried too much about him.

He looked into her tired eyes, not wanting to disappoint her.

"There was one girl there that seemed interesting, but I don't even know her name. I think she is a friend of Jessica Danley. I saw them the other..."

"Jessica? I'm friends with her mother. I could ask her and see..."

Saxton stood up, rubbing the sore spot on his chest.

"No, Mom! I don't need you to be trying to hook me up again. I'm not one of the characters in your books."

"I know, I know. I just thought I could get a little information for you and pass it on," his mother replied with a wink.

He headed to his room, somewhat annoyed, "That's okay, Mom. I got it covered."

Saxton closed his bedroom door, wanting to disappear. He knew his mother meant well, but she still got on his last nerve with the girl stuff. It was as though she was trying to hook him up with someone just to cure her own loneliness.

He removed his shirt, not really wanting to see what could have possibly caused him so much pain. He faced the mirror above his dresser, his eyes closed to his image.

He opened his eyelids slowly, dreading seeing the mark that appeared after the incident at McGuire's.

He expected to find blood under his shirt. But the scar, which was beginning to look more like a paw print, was just slightly red.

As he looked at his reflection, his mind turned to the girl at the dance that had placed her hand on his shoulder.

What was it about her that seemed so special?

It was as if he were mesmerized by her presence. However, it made no sense that every time he got near her something seemed to happen.

Could this mystery girl be the cause?

Surely not!

As he finished undressing, he glanced at the mark on his chest one more time. He knew where he would be headed in the morning, The Mystics' Book Emporium.

Chapter Two

Licah reached out from under her blanket and grabbed hastily for her ringing phone.

"Hello?" she answered groggily.

She had been up half the night, concerned about the situation with the guy at the dance.

"Hey, chick. You want to go to Alfredo's and grab some breakfast? I'm dying to tell you what happened with Sam last night!"

Licah stifled a groan.

Jessica was such a morning person. It was Saturday and the girl was calling her at seven.

But she knew better than to blow her off, she would just call back in half an hour to see if Licah had changed her mind.

"Sure," she offered, "let me grab a shower and I'll be there around eight."

Licah stumbled into the bathroom and started the spray to a degree below lava temperature.

She unclothed herself and stared into the mirror.

The mark had darkened a little since the night before.

She looked at it closely and decided it looked a little like a paw print.

She had no idea why it was there.

Maybe Jessica would have an idea.

She made it to Alfredo's at five minutes before eight.

Jessica was perched at a wrought iron table on the patio of the little café.

She waved at her and sat down with her friend.

"We so got to third base last night," she began.

Jessica was like that, straight and to the point, and it was always about her.

Licah ordered a croissant and a cup of orange juice while Jessica rattled on about Sam's kissing abilities, among other things.

Jessica finally took a breath and drank the rest of her coffee.

Licah started to mention the mark when Jessica started up again, but this time, Licah was more interested in the subject.

"Can you believe how weird Saxton was acting last night? He just ran out on Jack. And the way he acted at the coffee shop a few weeks ago?"

Saxton. So that was his name.

31

"What's his deal?" Licah asked.

Jessica paused for a moment, probably stunned that Licah was showing an interest in her rambling.

"I don't really know. He's never acted like that before."

Licah took a deep breath and seized the rare moment of silence.

"You remember that day at the coffee shop when he ran out?"

Jessica rolled her eyes.

"Of course, what a douche bag."

Licah tried not to groan at her friend's stuck-up demeanor.

"I ended up with this weird burn or mark on my chest, and I'm not sure what it is."

Jessica's nose turned up.

"Eww."

Licah pulled the neckline of her sweater over and showed her.

"You look like a dog stepped on you!" she shouted.

Licah looked around, but most of the breakfast crowd had cleared out.

She pulled her sweater back into place.

"What do you think it is?" she asked, wondering why she was even bothering with it.

Jessica shrugged.

"When did it happen?"

Licah took a deep breath.

"That's just it. I think it happened when he was standing at our table at McGuire's. As soon as he came near us, I felt my skin burn right where this mark is now."

Saxton awoke to an extremely brisk Saturday morning. He exited his bedroom with fresh clothes in hand and headed for the shower.

As the warm water pelted against his long frame, he looked down at the strange burn.

It seemed to have faded in color overnight. He could still trace his finger over the outlines of the oddly shaped marks.

He hoped that George would have some answers.

He grabbed a towel, dried off, and located a pen and a sheet of paper.

He went back in the bathroom and placed the paper over his mark and carefully traced the circles.

He held up the paper and looked at it in the light.

It really did look like some sort of animal paw print.

He finished dressing and stuck the sheet into his pocket.

He looked around the house and realized his mom must be at work.

Not feeling the need to eat breakfast, he gathered up his jacket and keys, sprang out the front door and into his car.

The drive to Memphis was not a short one. It gave Saxton time to think.

Maybe he should have taken his mom up on the offer of quizzing Jessica's mom for information on the girl at the dance.

After all, she was incredibly beautiful.

It was obvious that she hadn't grown up in Parker's Ridge.

Her dress and hairstyle spoke volumes on that subject, but that voice... When she spoke to him at the dance it really had stuck in his head.

Her voice was so alien and yet so alluring.

He had to find out more about her.

Upon arriving at The Mystics' Book Emporium, he looked around to see if there were any other customers in the shop.

He didn't want to be seen or heard asking some of the odd questions that he hoped George could answer.

He was used to keeping things to himself and wanted nothing to do with rumors leaking back to Van Pelt High.

After surveying the parking lot, he exited his car and walked up to the corner shop.

The building was old and brittle. The bricks looked as though they had been showered with shotgun fire. Whole pieces of rock and mortar had been chipped away by weather and time and were strewn across the sidewalk here and there.

He looked at the old glass door. There were various ads and pictures taped to the inside. He noted the hours of the business on the sign and entered, the door dragging across the floor with a loud scrape.

Saxton entered the bookshop cautiously. He took in all the tomes lining the wall, floor to ceiling.

Old ceiling fans rotated at a snail's pace about the large room. They circulated the aroma of dried, yellowed paper and lavender incense.

The area was lightly lit, not like your normal book retailer or library. There was a row of antique tables at one end of the shop with wooden chairs placed in pairs. Each table had a small, green reading lamp placed in the center.

Saxton could see the smoke trails of several large sticks of incense rising in front of the shadowy lamps.

The old floor creaked under his weight. He could see a thin coating of dust in the rarely traveled areas of the varnished wood floor.

Behind a tall counter, he could see George thumbing at a large blue book. His fingers barely touching the pages, which told Saxton the book was very old.

He walked up to George, facing him at eye level. The man was completely bewitched by what he was reading.

"Ahem," Saxton uttered quietly.

"Saxton, what brings you here on a Saturday? It's been quite a while since you have been in."

The older man took off his reading glasses and placed them on his desk.

He looked to be about fifty years of age, but Saxton considered him to be much older.

His salt-and-pepper hair was wiry and unbrushed. Saxton could see that he had a few teeth missing behind his dry lips.

"Geo, I'm thinking of doing some research on..." he paused. He didn't even know what to call it.

"Well, on what, son? I know you didn't drive all the way from Parker's Ridge and not know what you came out here to look up." The older man straightened in his high seat.

"Um, well. I'm not sure what to call it. I've come across some strange markings, and I was hoping you might be able to identify them."

Saxton felt like a fool, but he knew that if anyone might know anything about the mark on his chest, Geo would. The man was a walking encyclopedia of odd things.

Saxton motioned for Geo to lean forward, "Can we go over there for a second?" He pointed to area just behind the row of tables.

Geo hopped down from his seat. The man was barely five feet tall.

He marched over behind the tables. Saxton followed, slumping down to the old man's level.

Geo turned one of the chairs around and sat down, the chair's back leaning slightly against the reading table.

The incense smoke formed a halo around his head.

Saxton stood facing him, his hands at his sides.

"What is so secret you couldn't ask me over there?"

Saxton dug the sheet of paper out of his pocket, unfolding it carefully. He handed it to Geo who realized his reading glasses were still on his desk.

Paper in hand, Geo walked over to get his glasses.

The sound of the front door scraping across the floor startled Saxton.

Jessica!

Saxton dove behind the row of tables, crouching out of sight.

"Hey Geo, you really should get that door fixed. It's getting harder and harder to get in here."

Placing the paper down next to his glasses, Geo greeted his new customer.

"Hello, Jessica. What can I get you today?"

"I was checking if you got that book I ordered on the Chinese Zodiac," she said as she walked up to him.

Saxton couldn't make her out very well from his position, but her hair seemed to have more purple in it than normal.

He didn't recall seeing her at the dance last night. Since he was only there for less than fifteen minutes, she probably had come in after he had left.

"Yes, my dear, it came in. Hold on a moment, and I will fetch it for you." He scurried away to a small side room.

While she waited, Jessica surveyed the room, looking at the lethargic ceiling fans and the enormous collection of books.

Her jaw was moving slightly as she chewed on a piece of bubble gum.

Her gaze reached Geo's desk and fixated on the piece of paper. She slid it to within her vision and gasped.

Saxton tried to get a good look at her, but one of the bookracks blocked his view.

She pushed the paper back and headed for the exit.

Geo came out of the small room with a book in his hand, just in time to see her tug the door open and hurry away.

"Wait, I found the book you ordered..." He shook his head and carried it back into the storeroom.

Geo returned to his desk and collected the paper and glasses. He ambled back to Saxton, still shaking his head slightly.

"Okay, son, let me sit and take a look at this." He stared at it intently, trying to understand why Saxton wanted to be so secretive.

Saxton leaned over the graying man, "Have you ever seen anything like that before?"

Geo scratched the stubble on his chin, obviously in deep thought, "Can't say that I have, although, it looks a lot like a wolf track."

Saxton was bewildered, "A wolf track?"

"It's possible, but I will need to do some serious looking if you want me to figure it out. May I keep this drawing?"

Saxton stiffened. He didn't want anyone else finding out about his newly placed mark.

Quickly relaxing, he decided the drawing wouldn't be much of a giveaway.

"Yes, but please don't show it to many people. I don't want anyone to know I asked you."

"Sure, son."

That was one good thing about Geo; he rarely asked questions and respected a person's privacy.

He shook Geo's weathered hand and started for the door, leaving the drawing behind.

Just as he went to leave, he looked back at Geo, "You want me to give that book to Jessica? We go to school together."

George looked at Saxton curiously.

He could tell that Saxton had something up his sleeve to volunteer the book's delivery.

Geo grinned at him, "Sure, son, but if she doesn't get it, you owe her fourteen ninety-nine."

He retrieved the book from the small stockroom and handed it to Saxton.

His eyes had a strange twinkle in them that made Saxton frown.

Walking out the door, he wondered just how observant George Riner really was.

Licah went back home after a long morning at Alfredo's with Jessica and cleaned her room.

It didn't take long, as she was a bit of a neat freak anyway.

She sat down at her desk and grabbed her journal. The only true friend she'd ever had. She turned to a new page and began to write.

My impetuosity consumes me,
As loneliness pervades,
Why must I ensure,
These ever changing ways.

Why must I be the same,
When I know I am alone,
And wander through this life,
With no place to call my own.

I am my own person,
With loves, hopes, and dreams,
But in the eyes of others,
Things are never what they seem.

41

Should I stand and wait,
For someone to shut the door?
No, I can't and I won't,
This sorrow nevermore.

She clapped her journal shut and rubbed her temples.

The last thing she needed was to sink into depression.

Her mother wasn't doing well at all. She knew she had been going to the doctor while she'd been at school.

Licah helped balance the checkbook, and doctor co-pays were coming out fairly regular.

She worried the cancer had returned.

She didn't know if she could deal with her mother going through chemo again.

The last time, she lost all her hair, and Licah had been told to collect it to ensure no one used it for nefarious purposes.

Licah wasn't jaded. She knew there were unexplainable things out there. Coming from a Romanian gypsy family, it wasn't hard to see.

She just grew tired of her mother's superstitions and random beliefs about such simple things.

Sometimes she just wanted the impossible.

Sometimes she just wanted to be normal.

It was late afternoon when Saxton passed the sign reading, "Welcome to Parker's Ridge, founded 1822, Population, 10,777."

He drove in the direction of McGuire's Brewhouse on a hunch that Jessica would be there.

Carlos' place was in the older part of the city, in the historical town square. The coveted location was probably how Carlos managed to charge so much for his brews.

Downtown, with its sidewalks and wrought-iron light posts lining the streets, was Saxton's favorite part of Parker's Ridge, second only to the park.

When his mom was little, downtown was all there was to the sleepy township.

It certainly had more of a historical vibe than the strip malls and supercenters strewn about on the eastern part of the city.

Saxton pulled his car into one of the empty spots in the square.

He approached the coffee shop and tried to look into the window, but the glass was too darkly tinted.

Book in hand, he took a deep breath and pulled open the brass-handled door.

Saxton let the door shut behind him.

He spied around the room until he found what he was looking for.

There, in the back corner, sat Jessica Danley.

Her black and purple hair seemed to suck all the color out of the otherwise cheery corner.

Her solid black jacket had various pins and buttons decorating it, making her look like a goth pincushion.

She was alone and sipping on some iced coffee, her eyes staring blankly at something only she could see.

Saxton walked up to her, a sheepish grin on his lips, "Jessica, you forgot your book at Mystics'. I told Geo I would give it to you."

His voice pulled her out of her thoughts, and she slowly looked up his long body, seeming to scan him down to the bone.

Her eyes stopped on the book and locked onto it.

Saxton shifted his weight, wishing to turn into liquid and flow out the front door.

Jessica finally spoke, "How'd you know it was mine?"

Saxton tried to think of a convincing lie, but nothing came to mind.

44

He cleared his throat and half whispered, "I was there when you came to get it. I guess you didn't see me."

She finally looked up at his face, her dark blue eyes seemed to almost gleam, "No, I didn't see you. You say Geo told you to give it to me?"

Saxton swallowed hard and nodded his head in her direction. He could feel his palms begin to sweat.

Her brow tightened, "Then why haven't you given it to me yet?"

She snatched the book out of his hand and then proceeded to ignore him.

He mustered up enough courage to say, "I was just worried why you ran outta there so fast. What happened?"

"You wouldn't get it, Sax."

"Try me, you might be surprised."

Saxton sat down in front of her, his arms propped on the table.

She glared at him, as if wondering who had given him permission to sit there.

"Look, I'm waiting for my friend, Licah."

Saxton looked at her strangely; he had heard that name before.

"Do I know her?" he asked.

Jessica rolled her eyes.

"She's the gypsy girl."

Saxton almost jumped from his seat, "She's supposed to be here?"

She rolled her deep blue eyes again, "She was supposed to be here about ten minutes ago."

Saxton straightened in his seat and tried to keep his eyes locked on hers.

It was difficult to do.

She was very overpowering to him, and he found it hard to look straight at her.

"You wanna talk about it?"

"With you? Not really, no! You probably just wanna try to get in my pants."

Saxton's face hardened. "No, I...I just wanted to ask you what was wrong at the book store," he lied.

He finally had to break his gaze with her. She seemed far too hostile to talk about much of anything.

He looked at the floor and spotted one of her pins from her coat.

He reached down to pick it up, and his shirt shifted to the left, revealing his scar.

Jessica's iced coffee went flying into Saxton's face. Her eyes went wide, and her mouth seemed to almost unhinge.

She screamed at him with an ultra-high frequency, "Oh my God! You have it too! Just like Licah!!"

She bolted toward the door, nearly flattening Carlos.

46

Her two toned hair fanned out as she ran toward the door, swung it open, and disappeared.

The half-a-dozen customers all looked at Saxton in amazement.

Carlos glared at him as the coffee dripped onto his nice clean floor, his dark skin nearly turning gray.

"I told you, man, stay away from the ones with the crazy hair!"

Saxton looked down at his coffee-drenched clothes, already sticking to him from all the sugar in the iced brew.

"Yeah Carlos, you warned me," was all he said.

Licah was pulling up to the coffee shop when she saw Jessica burst out of the door and run to her car.

The little yellow jeep quickly peeled out of the parking lot, and on a whim, Licah followed.

She was praying that she wouldn't get a ticket from the Parker's Ridge PD, but she was concerned about her friend.

Jessica spun into her driveway, nearly on two tires, and Licah pulled in behind her.

The punky girl got out of the jeep, pulling at her hair.

Licah jumped out and ran over to her.

47

"Jessica, what's wrong?" she yelled, grabbing her arm.

Jessica turned and gasped.

"I can't talk to you!" she yelled and ran toward the house.

Licah didn't pause as she ran onto the porch and blocked the door.

"What?" she asked, growing angry and more than a little frustrated.

After all the times she had sat listening to Jessica rattle on about herself, she deserved an answer.

"He's got one too! Get away from me!" she yelled, trying to move Licah out of the way.

Licah looked at her like she was crazy and asked, "Who? What are you talking about?"

Jessica stepped forward and pulled Licah's collar down.

"That. Saxton has one too! What is wrong with you, did you cast some kind of spell on him or something with your weird juju mother?"

Licah started as if she'd been slapped.

Strange as she may be, Jessica had never thrown Licah's heritage into her face before.

Jessica noted the look on Licah's face and began to cry.

48

"I'm sorry, Licah. I'm just freaked out."

Licah nodded and walked down the steps to her car.

"Please don't be pissed at me! I didn't mean that about your mom."

The hell she didn't.

Things spoken in jest were almost always what the person was really thinking at the time.

She got into her car and peeled out of the driveway.

She had to talk to her mom.

If they both had the mark, there was something strange going on.

She wished her grandmother lived closer than Virginia. She'd much rather go to her, but cancer or no cancer, she needed answers.

And she needed them now.

Saxton's sticky clothes lay on his bathroom floor, smelling of some really expensive java.

He soaped himself down and watched the syrupy coffee cascade down his body and gurgle down the drain of the shower.

Now, sugar-free, he paced his bedroom thinking about his meeting with Jessica.

What did she mean, "Just like Licah"?

He assumed she meant the mystery mark.

Circling his room, he eyed the image of his shirtless torso and arms in the dresser mirror.

Were his biceps larger?

Yeah, but why?

He certainly had not worked out lately, unless lifting Carlos' coffee mugs counted.

The mystery mark was still visible. The mirror drew his attention to it each time he circled past.

In mid-stride he stopped and came to the striking conclusion that his movements were that of an animal, stalking it's prey.

He looked in the mirror again and chalked it up to his imagination.

He fell onto the bed, back first.

He needed to talk to Jessica again. A chill went down his spine at even the thought of trying to talk to her.

She was seriously out there. He knew it would be best not to try it at the coffee shop again. God forbid she would be drinking one of Carlos' hot brews.

Saxton figured he would try talking to her at school.

He knew when and where she had math class. He was fairly confident that Licah was not in that class with her, and maybe he could get some sort of clue as to what was up.

Licah walked into the apartment to find her mother sitting in front of the television, watching a gushy love story.

She rolled her eyes and reached for the remote.

Her mother didn't even notice she was there until she turned the television off and stepped in front of it.

"Hey! I was watching that!" her mother exclaimed, throwing a pillow at her.

"I really need to talk to you," she replied, throwing the pillow back.

She walked over to the couch and sat next to her.

"Something strange is happening, and I need to know what it means."

Her mother's playfully irritated look turned serious.

Licah never talked to her about the old ways. That she was asking for her advice on something meant that whatever she had to say was serious.

"What is it, fiică?" he mother asked, calling her "daughter" in Romanian.

Licah pulled the neck of her poet shirt to the side and showed her the mark.

The print had scabbed over, but still looked angry and red around the edges.

She hadn't really known what her mother's reaction would be, but what happened was wholly unexpected.

Her mother dashed to the kitchen and grabbed a string of garlic from the counter.

She put it around her neck and muttered, "Duhul tigani" over and over.

She walked over to her daughter and poked Licah right on her mark.

"Ow! What was that for?" Licah exclaimed.

Her mother looked at her oddly and put her hands on her hips.

"When did this happen? Who is he?" her mother asked in a rush of Romanian that Licah barely understood.

"It happened a few weeks ago and who is who?" she fired back in English.

Her mother stiffened her spine and walked past her, nearly choking Licah with her garlic scent.

She picked up the phone and dialed.

She could hear her grandmother's sleepy voice, and she plopped down on the couch while her mother and grandmother fired back and forth in Romanian so fast, she couldn't understand a bit of the conversation.

Licah's mother slowly returned the phone to the cradle and pulled the strand of garlic from her neck.

"Fiică, you are going to live with your grandmother."

Monday morning arrived in a blurry buzz from the alarm clock. Saxton rolled over, trying to find the snooze button.

He accidentally turned the clock off and groaned. He knew if he tried to reset it, it would just cause him to wake up anyway.

Saxton got ready for school and sucked down a bowl of cereal while his mom looked on, wearing a strange grin that made his stomach clench.

He knew she had been up to something.

"So, you talked Jessica lately?"

Saxton spun around to stare hard at his mother, "Mom? What did you do?"

She sat her favorite coffee mug with the name, Amelia, etched in old English lettering on the kitchen table.

She batted her eyes at him, and her smile widened, "Oh, nothing," she said as she twisted away from him.

"Mom! Did you say something to her mother?"

She half turned back toward him, "I might have said something to her that you had mentioned Jessica's friend. Her name is Licah."

Saxton shook his head in disbelief. Jessica's mom was just as much of a big mouth as the lady in front of him.

He slammed his cereal bowl on the table with a deafening thud, "Damn it, Mother! You realize she is gonna say something to Jessica!"

She whirled to face him with a disapproving glance, "Well, what's the harm in that?"

"It's hard to explain. Look, I know it has been tough on you since dad passed away, but you're going have to stop trying to hook me up with every available girl in Parker's Ridge."

He grabbed up his coat and started for the door. "I just don't need your help in this."

As he slammed the door, his mother picked up her coffee cup.

Before taking a fast sip she whispered, "Just trying to help."

Saxton stood in one of the freshman halls at Van Pelt High School. The white and brown walls reminded him of Neapolitan ice cream missing strawberry.

He kicked his gray and white trainers on the speckled floor, and he leaned next to the door to Mr. White's math room.

He wished the bell would ring. He knew he would catch hell if any of the teachers saw him skipping class.

Staring down, he absently contemplated the black fabric of his faded Jimi Hendrix shirt.

He played a thousand different scenarios through his mind of the conversation that was about to take place.

He knew Jessica's temperament all too well. As a matter of fact, most of the school knew it. So as he pondered, none of his solutions seemed very promising.

Saxton was balancing on the balls of his feet when the bell rang.

He popped down flat on his feet as the students filed out one by one.

He could just make out Jessica's form at the end of the line. Her beautiful hair flowed around her silky, pale neck.

Saxton shifted his position so she would not see him until she was out of the classroom.

He had no desire for her to think he was cornering her.

Jessica rounded the door sharply and collided into Saxton, her books flying in all directions.

Her eyes doubled in size at the sight of him.

"What are you doing in this part of the school, you freak?"

Jessica scrambled to pick up her books as the other students rubbernecked to see the commotion.

Saxton tried to help her retrieve her books, but she slapped his hand away.

"Jessica, listen, I need to find out why you got so freaked out at the coffee shop Saturday night. What did you see? Was it this?" He pulled his shirt to the left and revealed the scar. His long body bent over her so no one else could see.

Jessica looked and bolted straight up!

"Yes! That's what I saw. I don't know what your and Licah's deal is, but I want you two far away from me! You got that?"

Jessica stormed away, her black hair waving like a flag.

The other students just chuckled. Saxton figured they must be used to her theatrics by now.

Saxton straightened up to find Mr. White standing in his classroom doorway.

Saxton's cheeks turned scarlet with embarrassment.

Mr. White stood eye level with Saxton, "You're a little lost, aren't you, Lyall?"

"No, sir," Was all Saxton could squeak out as he turned and fled back to the senior's hall.

His next plan was to speak to Licah. His stomach rolled, and his scar slightly burned at the thought.

The three o'clock sun glinted in Saxton's eyes as he stood beside the long row of school buses on the edge of the dirty school parking lot.

He could hear the laughter of some of the students as they filed into the parking lot and onto the many buses.

Saxton had not bothered going to class. He'd left school and went to Stone Creek Park, about ten miles from the school, to chill.

It was his favorite place to go and think about music or girls.

It was a place of escape from all the troubles that came with being an eighteen year old in a small country town.

Of all of the areas in and around Parker's Ridge, the park felt like his true home.

Saxton popped back into reality as he saw Jessica walking out of the school. He knew they usually drove to school, but he had seen Jessica and Licah part ways at the buses a few times.

Saxton stepped back, so that Jessica would not see him. He saw with a groan that she was alone, walking to her jeep.

He wondered if the two girls had gotten into a fight about his accursed mark.

He scratched his chest. The mark was itching like a healing wound.

He spotted a girl from Jessica's math class heading toward the buses and quickly matched his step with hers.

He hoped she would have an answer to his question.

"Excuse me, would you happen to know Licah?"

The girl stopped and looked him up and down and smiled, "The girl from New York? I don't know her, but I had a couple of classes with her. Why?"

"I'm trying to find her. Do you know if she has left school already?"

The girl flashed a quick frown, "No. The rumor is her mother sent her off to live with her grandmother over the weekend. No one knows why. The story seems all kinda weird to me. Everyone calls her the gypsy girl. But, like I said, I don't really know her."

The girl continued to walk toward her bus, leaving Saxton with his mouth hanging open. "So she left?" he thought to himself.

It made no sense at all.

As Saxton ambled to his car, he moved his collar to look at the mark on his chest.

When he looked down, he knew why it had been itching so. The scab had flaked off, and the mark had faded to a light pink and was as smooth as the rest of his freckled chest.

Chapter Three

Manhattan, New York – 2012

The Vanderbilt Building always reminded Licah of a stack of Jenga blocks waiting to come tumbling down. It was a skyscraper of over eighty floors, but it was beige. Beige.

She shook her head as she walked into the revolving door and headed toward the bank of elevators at the end of the enormous lobby.

She adjusted the strap of her laptop case as she waited for an available lift door to open.

She could see her image in the metal door's reflection.

Her cream-colored business suit accentuated her tanned skin.

Her black hair was twisted up into a becoming chignon, but she felt like such a fake.

Gone were her gypsy skirts and poet shirts.

She was now a professional. A published author.

Her latest book, *Romanian Superstitions,* had made the New York Times Best Sellers List, her fourth book to make the list.

She supposed she should be excited, but her muse had dried up.

It was time to take a break.

She got on the elevator with two gentlemen, both turning to admire her before asking politely which floor she needed.

"Thirty-four, please," she stated, avoiding their gaze.

The man closest to the controls pressed the button indicating her floor.

The rising elevator was awkwardly silent. Both men continued to stare at her with those ogling eyes most men get when eyeing prey.

She was so tired of New York. Everyone wanted something from you.

She got out on her floor, leaving the two gents behind to whisper about her.

JoAnna Pennington, her editor, had an office at the end of the western corridor.

Rutland, Cochran, and Pennington Books dominated the entire floor and the one above.

She walked briskly down the hall, waving at familiar faces and saying polite hellos to those who acknowledged her.

JoAnna's secretary greeted her with a nod, picking up the phone to announce her presence.

She started to take a seat in one of the plush chairs in the waiting area when Gwen said with a smile, "Ms. Pennington will see you now, Ms. Daciana."

"Thank you, Gwen," she replied with a return smile, turning to walk to JoAnna's door.

Before she could twist the knob, her friend walked out of her office and gave her a warm hug.

"It's so good to see you, Licah. Do you want some coffee or tea?" she asked.

JoAnna was a small woman, barely topping five feet, but her shapely curves were in all the right places.

She was a powerhouse when it came to promoting books and a veritable handbook of grammar.

Licah felt lucky to have her.

"I'd love some tea," she responded, following her friend into the room.

JoAnna leaned out the door.

"Gwen, can you make up two cups of chamomile, please?"

"Of course, Ms. Pennington."

JoAnna closed the door as Gwen rushed to the small kitchen down the corridor.

Her friend was also as blunt as she could be. Instead of making niceties, she got right to the point.

"Still no new material?" she asked.

Licah shook her head and took a chair in front of JoAnna's massive mahogany desk.

"I'm as dry as a bone, Jo. I need to get away for a while."

JoAnna sat in her enormous leather chair, which Licah had always thought should make her look like a child, but JoAnna's posture and demeanor always made her appear larger than life.

"Licah," she began gently, "we've worked together for ten years. You've more than proven your worth here. If you have writer's block, take some time off. Go somewhere you feel calm."

She nodded.

She had been toying around with the idea of returning to Parker's Ridge. Out of all the places she had flitted to over the years, the small Tennessee town seemed ideal for a getaway.

"I have somewhere in mind," she offered, pulling out a printout of prices for cabins in Stone Creek Park.

JoAnna looked over the papers and nodded.

"I'll give you three months," she said, "putting the papers in a folder on her desk marked with Licah's name."

Licah's eyes widened.

"Don't look at me like that. You've made tons of money for me with your novels, and it's time we gave a little back. An all expenses paid vacation to Tennessee."

Licah knew better than to look a gift horse in the mouth.

Parker's Ridge, Tennessee - 2012

Saxton sat with his back to his desk facing the window, so he could admire the early lights of dawn. He could just make out the sun's glow seeping through the open, wooden mini-blinds.

Steam rolled from the stony rim of his coffee mug as if inviting him to take another sip.

Saxton's gaze never faltered. He looked upon the land outside like a cautious wild beast waiting for his prey to bound over the hill.

Saxton wore his standard khaki uniform and jacket that he had worn to work the past fifteen years.

On his desk, the letters read: Saxton Lyall, Stone Creek Park Ranger. The golden finish of the letters was darkened with time and age.

Saxton watched as two cardinals fought against the stiff, autumn air.

He thought to himself, "It'll be a while before I'll see you two again, won't it guys?"

Saxton rolled around in his chair to face forward. His coffee was still steaming in his left hand.

He loved his job as a ranger. He could be wrapped within nature every day.

An additional perk of his job was that he got to live within the park; and now that he was the head ranger, he had the luxury of his choice of the cabins.

His eye had always been on the cabin at the far west end of the grounds and that was where he'd made his home.

Saxton had been lucky. When one of the oldest rangers in Stone Creek Park had retired in ninety-six, Saxton's mother had used her hometown status to convince the city to hire him, her nosiness and consistent busy-body attitude finally paying off.

He chuckled at the thought of his now wiry white-haired mother and went back to his coffee.

Saxton picked up the newspaper on his desk and scanned the headlines.

He heard the front door to the lobby open and close. He didn't even bother to look up, he knew who it was.

Samantha Taylor poked her head into Saxton's office door, "Morning boss!"

Saxton lowered his paper and grinned at the young brunette, "Morning Sam! How did you rest?"

Sam stepped into his office, "Eh, not all that great. Still got something bangin' around in the attic. Thinkin' it's a raccoon. Every time I get up there to look, whatever it is, it runs off. Still can't figure out how it's gettin' in."

Saxton motioned for Sam to sit in the chair opposite him. She waved off his invitation, "Oh no, I gotta catch up on stuff at my desk."

Saxton could see the awkwardness in her eyes.

It had been pretty apparent for several months now that Sam had a bit of a crush on her boss.

He didn't mind.

She was an attractive woman. Her ample, brown locks flowed down her long, fair neck and covered her petite shoulders.

That he was ten years her senior didn't bother him. What did bother him was what might happen if he allowed himself to have feelings for her.

The mark on his chest was a constant reminder of what could happen, and it was not a risk he was willing to take.

Saxton looked into her large, youthful brown eyes, "Sam, you take this job way too seriously. I promise the park will still be here if you don't answer the phone on the first ring."

Sam giggled, her eyes flashing. She had been working at the park for only a few months, but she was already a great worker and a positive, morning fixture in the office.

As if responding to Saxton's words, the phone rang.

Sam wheeled around and said in a mocking tone, "You see, you already got me behind this morning."

Saxton laughed as Sam bounced out his office door.

"Good Morning. Stone Creek Park Office."

Saxton could barely make out the rest of what she was saying, but it sounded like it could be someone wanting to rent a cabin.

"Hmm...odd," he thought to himself. Not exactly the time of year for people to be looking for cabins.

Saxton took a long drink of his coffee and continued perusing his paper.

He missed Carlos' special brew.

Licah had expected cabs to be waiting in front of the Memphis International Airport, but was disappointed when she realized that she would have to rent a car.

She walked back into the airport and went to the rental kiosk.

"Hey there. How can I help you?" a young girl asked with a wave.

Her accent grated on Licah's northern ears, but she figured she was going to have to get used to it eventually.

"I'd like to rent a small SUV," she responded, pulling out her credit card.

"Are you Leah Dasheena?" the girl asked, looking down at her computer.

Licah closed her eyes at the mispronunciation of her name, and nodded.

"Rutland, Cochran, and Pennington have already made a reservation for you," she said, handing her a set of keys with a Tennessee Vols rubber emblem hanging from them.

Licah took the keys and looked at the paperwork the girl handed to her.

A Jeep Wrangler.

Licah almost laughed out loud at the absurdity of it, but she signed the papers anyway.

"Just go down there to the right after you leave the doors. The lot is sectioned off with road cones. Bernard is down there in the little shack, and he'll show you to your car."

The girl's accent was so heavy, Licah had trouble understanding it until she ran it through her mind again.

Culture shock at its finest.

Saxton sauntered from his comfy office. No need to rush. Campers would not be out in full force that time of year.

Not that he minded the silence.

This was the time he got to enjoy the park himself.

No more repairing the various necessities broken by the partygoers in the townhouse.

No more going and gathering up the various wild animals out of the cabins, because those yanks had never been away from the concrete and towering heights of city life before.

Mainly though, he could work on the research that had absorbed his life for over fifteen years.

His research of *Blestemul Vârcolac de Dragoste.*

The Romanian phrase passed through Saxton's mind, and he remembered that humid, summer day in ninety-six.

What he had learned that day had changed his life forever.

Saxton hurried into Mystics' Book Emporium and shouted, "Geo! I got your message."

Geo moseyed out of one of the rooms lining the back wall. A strong smell of lavender incense and cigarette smoke wafted around him.

Geo extended his right hand and shook Saxton's vigorously, a large grin on his aged lips. "So glad to see you, Sax! You have not been in for months."

"I've been working. It is weeks like this at Stone Creek Park that make me wish I was in high school again."

Geo's smile only grew wider, "I finally have some information for you on the drawing you gave me nearly three years ago." He held up a dog-eared sheet of paper and slightly waved it in the air.

The two of them walked to Geo's tall desk and sat down. A thick tome sat next to a green tinted reading lamp.

Geo switched on the bulb and unfolded the yellowing paper. Saxton saw there were words written under his old tracing.

Blestemul Vârcolac de Dragoste

Geo pointed to the strange words and looked into Saxton's eyes, "This is written in Romanian, right? You have any clue what it says?"

Saxton shook his head in honesty, "Not a clue."

Geo slid the paper closer to him and looked down at the words as he translated, "In English it reads: 'The Werewolf Curse of Love.' Now listen to me very carefully."

Geo reached for the large book and opened it to a marked page.

His weathered finger traced a section as he read, "This curse goes back to Romania in the eighteenth century. The legend states that a woman there was rejected by her lover, because of an arranged marriage. In her love-sickened grief, she cursed her lover and killed his bride-to-be. Upon being cursed, her lover turned into a werewolf and carried a mark, or burn, as it is sometimes addressed. That is the mark, here," he pointed to Saxton's old tracing.

Geo's eyes glowed with intrigue.

71

Saxton shifted in his seat, his pulse pounding in his ears. He tried to lick his dry lips, but his mouth had become completely parched.

"It is also believed that descendants of the estranged couple will carry the mark. If a descendant of one comes into contact with the other, the mark will appear on each of them. According to the legend, the male will then turn into a werewolf anytime he is in the girl's presence."

Saxton started to become dizzy, his mind racing with too many questions. He knew he carried the mark, and that must mean Licah had it for the same reason.

Saxton braved a question, "Does it say if the girl also turns into a werewolf?"

Geo shook his head, "It just says 'the male'. It says nothing about the female turning. But, she will carry the mark."

Saxton thought in desperation, "Is there some sort of cure for the curse?"

"According to this, there is believed to have been a cure once upon a time, but there is no information here."

Saxton pulled the book to him. The dust on its cover smeared the desktop. He stared at the book, hoping it would give him some comfort.

He looked at the passage again and had noticed the page number. It read '274'. The next page, however, read '277'.

"Geo! There is a page missing!"

Geo snatched the book back, his eyes focusing on the corner.

"Well I'll be damned. There is!"

"Maybe the cure was listed on the missing pages," Saxton prayed.

Geo glided his fingers along the books inside crease, feeling the thin, jagged edge of the missing sheet, "That's a possibility. This book is very old, one hundred and fifty years, at least. There is no telling where that page is now."

"What else does it say?"

Geo looked closer at the page, "If the female is already betrothed upon the two meeting, the man will take whatever measures required to destroy his rival. He will go to any lengths, even to the point of the loss of his own life."

Saxton collapsed backward, almost toppling his chair, his mind unable to comprehend his fate. He ran his clammy hand across his forehead to wipe away the feverish sweat.

"What am I going to do?" he thought to himself.

"This is completely insane! This just doesn't happen in real life!"

Geo looked at him. His forehead pulled his bushy eyebrows together, "Now don't be so sure! There are lots of things that happen in this world that we know nothing about."

Saxton considered showing the mark to George, but quickly dismissed that idea.

Geo pointed to Saxton's tracing, "Now, son, I usually don't dig into people's private business, but where did you find this sketch?"

Saxton tried to think of a good lie, "Uh, I went into one of the old closed-down schoolhouses and found it in the cloak room."

He hoped that sounded convincing. After all, those old buildings (one being there since the town had been founded) had been closed for decades waiting to be renovated as historical landmarks and were common prowling grounds for anyone interested in local history.

Geo's expression was one of disbelief. He studied Saxton's face and his eyes narrowed.

Saxton met his gaze and quickly looked down at the old book in front of him. Saxton knew his lie was not believed.

Changing the subject to break the tension, Saxton asked, "Where did you find the book?"

"A collector found it in the area of the old British-American settlement of the Condeskeag Plantation located in Bangor, Maine."

Saxton looked at him inquisitively, wanting to know more.

"It was the first settlement in what became Bangor. The first settlers started the plantation in seventeen hundred sixty-nine. He said it came from the site of an old sawmill."

Saxton stood to leave. He couldn't hear any more of the insanity, at least not that day.

He shook George's hand, thanked him, and headed for the door.

Geo spoke up, "Hey, you want your sketch back?"

Saxton glanced over his shoulder, "Keep it, I have another."

Saxton was snapped back into reality when his secretary spoke to him, "Boss, looks like we may have a little business coming in after all."

Saxton groaned at Samantha, "You're kidding?"

"No, I just got a call that a girl is coming in from New York for a three month stay. The reservation was made by a publishing company up there."

"New York, huh? Well, make sure the squirrels stay out of her cabin. She might think it's a new breed of super-rat," he chuckled as he took his hat from its hook and headed outside.

He stood on his office porch and took in a deep breath of the cooling September air, his lungs filled to capacity.

He gazed at the fallen leaves signaling autumn's return. The trees, with their many colors, eased his mind and calmed his worries. He loved his job, simply because of that.

His eyes surveyed his familiar surroundings. He took in one more cleansing breath, but instead of calm, he felt an ancient, but all too recognizable burn on the left side of his chest.

The drive from Memphis hadn't taken as long as Licah had thought it would.

Her cellphone rang, and she reached into her bag to retrieve it, keeping her eyes on the road.

"Hey Jo," she answered after a quick glance at the screen.

"It's Gwen, Jo's in a meeting. I just wanted to let you know that your reservations have been made for the cabin. There's a girl named Samantha at the front desk who should accommodate you."

Licah smiled as she passed the sign for Parker's Ridge.

A few numbers had been added to the end of the population number, but other than that, it was exactly the same as she remembered.

"Thanks Gwen, I really appreciate it," she said, turning into a gas station.

"Yes, Ms. Daciana. Is there anything else I can help you with?"

Gwen was always so formal with her.

"No, that's absolutely perfect. Tell JoAnna that I will be in touch soon."

"Yes, ma'am," Gwen replied and hung up.

Licah pulled the jeep up to the pump and climbed out.

The service station had been updated, new lighting had been installed, and there were four pumps now, instead of two.

A man walked out of the service station. He wore greasy blue coveralls, and the name embroidered on his chest was Jack.

"May I help you?" he asked in a friendly manner.

Licah smiled and shook her head. Parker's Ridge had to be the last place on Earth that still had a full service gas station.

She glanced up and noticed she had pulled up to the pump with the full service sign, instead of the self-service row closer to the road.

Oh well. What's a few more cents a gallon?

"If you don't mind cleaning the wind shield and filling up, I'd like to run into the ladies' room."

She turned on her heel, grabbing her purse. She glanced back and caught the mechanic admiring her linen-covered backside.

Their eyes quickly met, and he smiled a wry grin. He looked at her for a few moments and recognition seemed to come to him.

"Hey, don't I know you?" he asked, walking a few steps closer.

Licah's heart tripped. She hoped he hadn't been one of the boys that had constantly called her gypsy girl in high school.

"I don't think so, but I did live here for a couple years until my freshman year of high school."

He looked at her closer and nodded his head.

"You're that Romanian chick."

Licah closed her eyes. Well, it was better than gypsy girl.

"I'm Jackson, we used to have chemistry together at Van Pelt."

He reached over to shake her hand, but quickly retracted it when he saw the long smudge of grease running across his knuckles.

"It's good to see you again. What are you doing here in Parker's Ridge?" he asked, wiping his hand on a greasy towel that had seen its better days.

She adjusted her purse strap and leaned against the jeep.

"I'm a writer. I'm just taking a little time off."

His eyes widened.

"A writer? My mom writes for the Parker's Ridge Herald, do you know her? If you're looking for work, I bet she could get you a job there."

Licah breathed deeply.

Small town mentality.

"No, I'm a novelist, not a journalist. I'm just taking a break between books. I thought I'd come back out here and see how things had changed."

Jackson grinned, "I'll be glad to show you around."

Licah smiled at the smooth attempt to get her to go out with him.

"That's okay. I'm a bit of a lone wolf."

Jack nodded and sheepishly started pumping her gas, "Let me know if you change your mind."

Licah nodded and headed to the service station's ladies' room.

She was washing her hands when she felt a sharp tingle strike the scar on her chest.

She hadn't thought about it in years.

She reached past her collar and felt it, and it was hot to the touch.

Strange.

Saxton returned to his office, his tracking boots covered in mud.

An aging bench sat next to the check-in lobby's door. He sat down and slid off his muddy footgear. Bending over to set his boots on the floor, he felt an itch nagging at his mark.

Saxton wondered why his scar would be drawing attention to itself after all these years.

He looked through the glass window at his secretary. Surely Samantha was not the cause.

He had stayed away from relationships as best he could since he had learned of the werewolf curse from Geo over fifteen years previous. It wasn't an easy feat, especially in his line of work.

Being a man in uniform had its perks and its downfalls when it came to relationships.

Even though it clearly stated Stone Creek Park Ranger on his badge, he would often be mistaken for a state policeman or government agent.

Saxton didn't, however, let his title or his uniform go to his head.

In many ways, he was still the same lonely and withdrawn teenager from nearly twenty years before.

Saxton stood and picked up his mud-caked boots. Retreating to his office, he gave Samantha a distracted smile as he closed the door.

It was time to make a trip to Memphis.

He quickly tossed his muddy boots on an old dirty rug in the back of his closet, hung up his ranger jacket, grabbed a change of clothes from the top shelf, and headed to his personal bathroom.

Saxton needed to pay a visit to Geo and his mountains of age-scented books.

As Licah ascended the uphill climb into the entrance of Stone Creek Park, she passed a white park ranger truck and waved as she went by.

The moment her hand touched the steering wheel again, a sharp pain exploded on her chest.

She pulled to the shoulder and tried to catch her breath.

Her scar hadn't burned like that since she had been in high school at Van Pelt, right before her mother had shipped her off to Virginia.

She still didn't understand why her mother had been so worried she was in danger.

But, knowing her mother was sick, she hadn't argued.

She'd taken a midnight flight to Richmond and had lived with her Romanian grandmother until she'd graduated from college.

As soon as her mother had made arrangements to break the lease on their apartment and to have her medical records sent to Richmond Medical Hospital, she had come to live with them.

Not long after their move, her breast cancer had returned, and she had courageously chose to have a double mastectomy.

She still talked to her mother about once a week, and she, thankfully, remained cancer free.

Her mother and grandmother now lived in a little apartment together in Richmond.

Her mother worked as a psychic in a little shop a few blocks from the apartment.

She rubbed her chest again, but the burning had stopped.

She pulled back onto the small paved road and made her way up to the park office.

A young woman was sitting on a bench outside smoking a cigarette and reading a magazine.

She climbed out of the car and approached the building, watching the woman stub out her cigarette in an ashtray mounted to the bench.

"Hi there," she greeted, folding her magazine under her arm and presenting her hand.

Licah gave her a quick shake and said, "I'm Licah Daciana. Rutland, Cochran, and Pennington should have made reservations for a cabin for me today."

The young woman nodded and opened the door for her.

The cabin smelled of pine and a man's cologne she didn't recognize.

It had a homey smell to it and calmed her nerves after the episode in the jeep.

"My name is Samantha, but everyone here calls me Sam. You're going to be in the cabin at the far east end of the park. It's a nice two bedroom with a full kitchen. Since they just made your reservation, I haven't had time to run out there to make sure everything is in order, but there's a little café in town. If you'd like to go have an early supper, I'll run over there and take care of it."

Licah nodded and accepted a receipt and a set of keys.

"How are you going to get in?" she asked, putting the keys in the pocket of her suit jacket.

Sam smiled, "Oh, we have two sets to every cabin. This way you won't have to drop back in; you can just drive straight out and get settled."

Licah thanked her and walked back out to the jeep.

As an afterthought, she turned back around to see Sam lighting up again.

"Do you think you could put out the word for me not to be bothered?" she asked, hoping the woman wouldn't smoke in the cabin when she went to clean it up.

Sam nodded, blowing out a cloud of gray.

"You'll pretty much have the park to yourself. The Park Ranger has a cabin on the other end of the park, but all the other cabins are empty."

Licah smiled at that. It would be nice to have a little peace and quiet.

Saxton was on the higher end of concerned as he drove his white Ford F150 down the hill and out of the park.

His old scar had actually become warm to the touch.

For the first time in years, the old scar was acting up again, alternating between itching and burning.

He hoped Geo would know what to do.

It was time to confide in his old friend about the mark.

Saxton reached into his glove compartment and fumbled through it till he found a dried flower covered with wooly, white hairs.

It was Edelweiss, which was indigenous to Romania. Its Latin name, *Leontopodium alpinum*, was an adaptation of Greek and meant 'lion's paw'.

In his years of research it was the only thing he had found that might have an effect on his mark.

Saxton started to lift his shirt to place the wooly plant on his burning chest.

He could see a jeep in the distance, climbing the road. He saw the girl inside motion a wave as she passed.

Without warning, a fiery pain erupted in Saxton's left chest. His skin burned unbearably, his hair bristled, and his enlarging teeth pushed against his lips.

Saxton pushed the Edelweiss onto his throbbing chest and jammed on his brakes to come to a complete stop.

He checked in the rearview and saw the jeep had disappeared up the hill.

The last thing he wanted was a witness to the horrific event.

Saxton took a few deep breaths.

He could feel himself changing back before the transformation had taken a firm grip on him.

His labored breath slowed to a whisper, and his heart resumed its normal drumming staccato.

Saxton looked down at his torso.

He had crushed, no, nearly embedded the furry flower into his upper rib cage.

He pulled the plant away from his sweat-soaked body and studied the flattened texture of the plant with an eye of disbelief.

"Does this stuff really work?"

He had tried using it before, simply by holding it to his heart.

It had helped fade the mark to a mere shade under his average tone, but this was the first test during a real attack of the curse.

Saxton placed the disfigured flower back in its hiding place in the glove compartment.

He dare not toss it out or lose it. Edelweiss was fairly hard to come by as he had discovered trying to get the few flowers he had on hand.

Saxton let his foot off the brake of his truck and continued to the exit of the park.

As he pulled onto the highway, he raged an inward battle over what he was going to tell Geo when he arrived at the bookstore in the old part of Memphis.

He hoped his old friend was as understanding of odd things as his bookstore represented him to be.

McGuire's Brewhouse's atmosphere was exactly like she remembered it.

Carlos was still standing at the counter, cleaning what didn't need cleaning, and the place smelled heavily of java.

Licah perched on one of the counter stools, waiting for Carlos to notice her.

His hair was still closely shaven to his mocha colored head, but there was graying at his temples and small crow's feet next to his dark chocolate eyes.

"What can I get for you ma'am?" he asked with a brilliant smile.

Licah figured he didn't remember her. He had been out of school by the time they had moved to Parker's Ridge, and though she had frequented the coffee shop often as a teen, she'd never been much of a talker.

"White chocolate mocha and a McGuire club," she said, sitting down on one of the barstools.

"White, wheat, or rye?" he asked, writing down her order on a small receipt book.

"Rye," she responded, glancing around the room.

He had updated the lighting to those blown glass pendant lamps in every shade. They were strategically placed over the tables, creating a private atmosphere in each area.

The booth's seats had been reupholstered in a vibrant fabric matching the colors in the lampshades, each with variously colored mugs, steam climbing from their rims.

"The place looks good, Carlos," she said, spinning around as he presented her coffee.

He studied her face for a moment, trying to place her.

"Do I know you?" he asked, taking in her foreign features.

She stuck out her hand and shook his.

"Licah Daciana. I used to come here when I was a teenager."

The light in his eyes brightened.

"Yeah, you used to come in here with that Danley girl with the hair, right?" he asked, smiling once again.

Licah snickered and nodded.

"What brings you back to Parker's Ridge?" he asked while making her sandwich.

"I just thought I'd come down for a little R and R. I'm going to be here a few months," she responded, taking a long pull from her coffee.

Perfect, as always.

"A little R and R? Don't you have a job to go to?" he asked, placing her sandwich on a pristine square black plate with a pickle wedge on the side.

Licah laughed. Everyone in town was going to wonder that apparently.

"I'm a writer. My work comes with me, anywhere I go."

He placed the plate in front of her.

"What do you write?" he asked, leaning against the counter.

At least he wasn't offering her a job at the local rag.

"I write paranormal fiction and historical non-fiction novels."

He cocked his head to the side and nodded.

"You look the type that would do something amazing like that."

Licah felt a blush creep up her neck.

"Why's that?" she asked, taking a bite of her sandwich.

He looked down and scratched the back of his head.

"Sorry if that sounded like a come on. We just don't get many interesting people around these parts, as I'm sure you remember."

Licah nodded.

"This is great, by the way."

Carlos smiled and tapped the counter.

"I'll let you eat, Ms. Licah. Glad to have you back."

She smiled as he walked off.

Maybe this wasn't going to be so bad after all.

Chapter Four

Saxton pulled into the familiar parking area in front of The Mystics' Book Emporium.

He turned off the truck's engine and nervously stared at Geo's shop.

Time had not been friendly to the already aged building. All the cracks and imperfections that had always given the place character were now slowly eating it into oblivion.

The sun had set on Saxton about thirty minutes before the cityscape had engulfed him. The streetlights illuminated the uneven sidewalk, casting shadows at odd angles.

Saxton felt like the same nervous teen from so many years ago as he stepped from his truck onto the empty street filled with old city night sounds.

He caught a glimpse of himself in the side mirror, his skin mimicking the truck's ghostly white paint.

He approached the shop's timeworn entrance and pushed through the door, which still scraped against the floor as it struggled to swing open.

He hurriedly walked to Geo's favorite spot in the shop.

The tall desk was covered in papers, books, and drawings. He could make out the large print on the cover of one of the dust-coated books, *Nosferatu.*

He could hear voices echoing through the volumes of books in the building. One, he recognized as Geo's, the other, a girl's that sounded vaguely familiar; but he couldn't put a face with it.

Saxton spun around as Geo and a girl, all dressed in black, exited one of the back rooms.

He could make out her raven black hair curtaining her phantom pale face, an ever-present purple streak still flowing down her mane.

His gut tightened up at the sight of her.

"Well I'll be damned! Saxton Lyall! I figured your puppies had eaten you by now," Jessica Danley said in an all too familiar, mocking tone.

Saxton was so in shock, he didn't know if he should dive under Geo's desk, dash out the door, or hide in the book stacks.

"Jessica! So, you're still coming here too?"

As Jessica and Geo approached him, Saxton could make out her beautifully pale features. It was as if she had not aged a day since her senior year at Van Pelt High.

"Yep. I'm still hanging out with Geo from time to time. He keeps me outta trouble. Well, mostly."

Jessica came to stand in front of Saxton and embraced him with her comely figure.

He almost fell to the ground in fright. It would not have surprised him if a knife had been left in his spine after she broke the hug.

He would not have noticed, though. He was too numb with the fear of seeing his old schoolmate.

Geo's grin was too giddy and mischievous for Saxton's liking, "So, been a while for the both of you, I see."

Saxton looked at Geo with a tightened brow, "Yeah, it's been quite a while."

Geo placed another book on his tall desk, "Well, Jessica and I have a little finishing up to do. Would you give us another hour and then we can talk?"

Jessica waved her hand at Geo and grinned, "Oh, don't worry, G. You two go ahead. I'll be back in a few hours."

Jessica turned and strutted toward the door, her tall, black boots clicking on the old wooden floor.

When she arrived at the exit, she turned and looked at Geo, "Gonna be up all night anyway!"

She laughed, pulled the door open, and disappeared into the night.

Saxton shook his head, trying to clear his mind from the surrealness of seeing Jessica again.

Saxton thought to himself, "What the hell did she mean by, 'I figured your puppies had eaten you by now.'" He wondered if she had figured out what his mark meant.

He looked at Geo, his emotions written all over his face.

Geo stopped Saxton from speaking before he had the chance, "Don't look at me, I didn't tell her."

Saxton fell into the nearest chair, his eyes never leaving Geo's gaze, "Well, who exactly told you?"

Geo grinned like a sneaky child with their hand caught in the cookie jar.

"Son, I knew from the first moment you brought me the sketch to research. That mark is one of legend and the story you gave me about finding it in one of the old abandoned schoolhouses, no way!"

Geo took a breath and gave Saxton a knowing glance, "I have combed all over those buildings looking for historical information and an image of that mark would have been obvious to me, had I seen it."

Saxton shook his head, trying to shake all of it from his memory, "So you knew this whole time?"

Geo smiled, the corners of his mouth almost reaching his ears.

He quickly gathered up all the books and documents on his desk and placed them out of sight.

"Yes son, I have. But it's fine, and I will help you if I can. Actually, I have been helping you, and you haven't even known. Well, I should say, I have tried to help. There's just not a whole lot I have been able to find out. This Romanian curse has very little written about it, and the people who know of it are so tight-lipped, I really haven't got much to go on."

Saxton closed his eyes, deep in thought, "What about your friend who found the book explaining the curse, could he help?"

Geo shook his head as he hopped onto his desk chair, "No. He moved away. He shared very little information with me. He claimed to have little knowledge on the subject, but I think he was holding out on me."

Geo paused again, "However, he did give me all of his books when he left. I still have not been able to go through half of them. I've had so much going on, and he had so many books that I just haven't made it through them all."

Saxton ears perked up, "I can do it!"

Geo's grin returned, "You are more than welcome to. It is a lot of books, son. They've been sitting in one of the corners of my sorting room. Been piled up there for years, waiting for me to finish going through them before I sell them off."

Geo hopped back down from his desk and led Saxton to one of the back rooms.

Books were piled in every corner of the room. The smell of the old pages was a calming scent to Saxton's nerves.

Geo approached the corner that housed the biggest stack of volumes.

The stack, carefully covered in plastic, was three feet tall by three feet wide.

Saxton looked at the stack with trepidation.

Geo pulled away the covering and looked at Saxton, "Like I said, it's a lot of books."

Licah drove up to the cabin on the eastern end of the park and looked over the clapboard structure.

Could be worse, she supposed. It did have a nice deck on the back that jutted out from the house to overlook a small creek.

She got out of the jeep and grabbed her two bags of luggage.

She walked up the simple plank steps to the front porch and opened the squeaky screen door.

She inserted her key and unlocked the door. Expecting to get a whiff of cigarette smoke, she was pleasantly surprised to smell cinnamon apples.

She stepped into the front room and noted the stone fireplace with a basket of pinecones gracing the mantle.

Moving closer, she noticed the smell was emanating from them. She could see golden glitter embedded in the creases and figured they'd been dipped in an apple cinnamon solution.

Arranged near the fireplace, the couches were rustic and had seen better days, but looked comfortable and cozy.

Leaving her bags on the living room floor, she explored the small kitchen. She was pleased to find an updated stove, microwave, and refrigerator. Opening the cabinets revealed pots, pans, and dishes.

She left the kitchen and wandered down the hallway.

The first door on the left was a small room dominated by a full sized bed, nightstand, and a small desk with a lamp.

She walked farther and opened the door to the bathroom and sighed at the view of the deep claw-footed tub.

She would definitely be making use of that.

At the end of the hall, she discovered a larger bedroom with a king-sized bed covered in a white, goose-down comforter and two huge feather pillows.

Returning to the living room, it was the work of a moment to unpack her meager belongings and her laptop.

She allowed extra time with her second bag, removing a framed photograph of her mother, grandmother, and herself sitting on the steps of their old brownstone in Virginia.

Their resemblance to each other was uncanny, each having the same green eyes and dark curly hair, though the elder of the two had more gray.

The pain in her heart at the site of them was more than she had expected.

She missed them so much and hated that she had been too busy the last few years to spend a lot of time with them.

She took out a jasmine candle her mother had made for her using paraffin and real jasmine flowers and placed it on the nightstand in the master bedroom with the photo.

She reached into her bag to pull out the last item.

It was something her grandmother insisted she always carry with her, though she hadn't opened it in years.

It was a Romanian *vrajitoarei sac*, or witch's bag, containing a sage wand, a small bag of salt, healing herbs, and an amulet.

She sat it on the nightstand unopened and plopped down on the bed.

She was exhausted from the flight and the drive.

She would take a little nap and then open up the same blank document she had been staring at for weeks.

Maybe her muse would decide to come back now that she was away from the big city.

Saxton sat cross-legged in the back room of Geo's bookstore.

His hands were brittle with one hundred year old dust. After about the tenth paper cut, the texture of the old books' yellowing pages was losing its appeal.

The smell of the aged pages, which Saxton usually adored, was starting to make him nauseous.

His sinuses were full of decades of dirt, and his eyes felt as dry as the parched paper he was thumbing through.

Saxton looked at his watch under the small, green-glassed lamp that Geo had provided him.

It was one thirty in the morning. He knew he wasn't going to be conscious for much longer.

The words on the thousands of pages he had scanned were all becoming a jumbled blur in his mind.

It was nice that Geo had let Saxton stay as long as he had wanted so he could explore the various texts.

Geo's bookstore also doubled as his home.

Saxton knew his living quarters were up the spiral stairs near the back door, but he had never ventured up them.

Geo had already retired for the night. His last words before disappearing into his loft were, "Stay as long as you like, just make sure the door is locked when you leave."

Saxton had appreciated his kindness.

Due to his fatigue, he realized that any more research would be pointless. He stood and began restacking books, making sure to move all the volumes he had perused to the far right of the square pile. There was no need to dig through the same titles again on a return trip.

Saxton had pulled out a couple of books from the stacks to take back home with him, both of which being on Romanian history.

He reconstructed the book tower, and noticed a book on the bottom row, which managed to break through his wavy vision. The spine of the book read, *"Romanian Genealogy, 1720-1760"*.

From his research, he knew the origin of the curse was within that same time span. Maybe he could find a link to himself and the curse within its pages.

He snatched the book from the pile and stashed it with two others.

Once he finished restacking, he covered the stacks with the sheet of plastic and headed toward the front of the shop, scooping up the borrowed volumes as he passed.

The store was dimly lit as Saxton made his way to the door.

The shop was creepy enough during the day, but tenfold at two in the morning.

It seemed that every shadow twisted and turned as he marched by them.

It was almost as if they were turning to greet the invader as he passed through.

Saxton opened the door; exited, and pulled it closed with a large clack. He shook the door firmly to make sure it had locked.

Saxton looked up at the moon hidden behind clouds in the night sky. He could barely make out its orbed shape as he climbed into his truck and began his trek back to Parker's Ridge.

Licah watched as the thin gauzy curtains fluttered in the wind blowing through the window.

The king sized bed was nestled in the center of the room, and she lay on it with a familiar companion: her laptop.

She had taken a long, luxurious bath in the claw-footed tub and changed into a pair of gray fleece pants and a silky foam-green chemise.

She willed her attention to the laptop, looking at that ever-blank page, and twirled one of her curls around her right index finger.

She was so numb and uninspired.

A change of scenery is what she had been sure would kick her into gear, but so far... nothing.

She glanced back out the window and noted the beauty of the moon; its silvery light glinted off the glass and filtered down to the rough wooden floor.

She sat her laptop to the side. As she stood, it sank down into the plushness of the comforter.

The cool night chilled her bare feet as she padded over to the window and overlooked the forest.

The bark on the trees seemed nearly white as the moon filtered through the sparse autumn branches.

She took a deep, cleansing breath and closed her eyes.

You didn't get this kind of air in metropolitan areas. She had forgotten how good it felt.

Must be the smog to oxygen ratio or something.

Leaving the fresh air to be savored later, she ambled down the hall to the kitchen.

She opened the empty refrigerator and rummaged through the cabinets.

If she were going to stay there for three months, she would have to do some shopping the next day.

One hundred year old spaghetti noodles and baking soda just weren't going to cut it.

With a sigh, she returned to the bedroom, started some music on her laptop and crawled into bed to sleep.

As she nestled into the comforter, her hand brushed across her mark.

It still felt warm to the touch.

She hadn't thought about it in a very long time.

She hadn't thought of Saxton in a very long time.

Her mind pondered what had ever happened to the red headed teen.

There'd never actually been an opportunity for a proper conversation with him.

Oh well.

She allowed Tracey Chapman's husky voice to sing her to sleep.

She sank into oblivion before the second verse.

Saxton maneuvered his truck up the hill leading into Stone Creek Park.

"Whoa! Saxton," he said aloud when his truck hit the road's shoulder. "You've gotta get yourself some sleep!" His vision doubled and darted in all directions as he crested the hill.

The moon hung high in the night sky as Saxton pulled his Ford alongside his office building.

Sam had long since gone home. He could see her tray full of cigarette butts sitting next to the porch bench. "She must have been bored while I was away," he thought to himself.

Saxton continued to pull forward to make a round of the park.

Now was usually the time that folks were up to no good on the park's one hundred acres.

As tired as he was, he knew it would be in the best interests of the lone guest in the park for him to make a round or two.

Saxton's truck coasted down the next hill. He tried not to rev up the motor and wake up the park's new guest.

Since she planned to be there for three months, he knew that waking her up would not be the best way to impress his customer.

He saw her jeep sitting at her cabin. All the lights were off and the building was quiet.

He rolled his window down to listen for any unusual sounds nearby.

His ears perked up. He could hear a voice in the distance, near the girl's cabin.

Saxton eased from his truck; his feet hit the dirt roadway with a crunching thud. The stray, loose stones flew to the left and right of his large feet.

He crept closer, stealthily, like a stalking predator.

Edging nearer the cabin, he breathed a sigh of relief. It dawned on him the voice was from Leonard Cohen's *Hallelujah*.

He continued forward a few more steps to hear its soothing melody. Unexpectedly, his hand thrust up to clinch his chest, and his knees nearly buckled under his own weight.

"Ugh! What the...hell!" The burning from his mark was like that of a branding iron.

He staggered backward a few paces, and the burning subsided.

He decided to chance it again, and stepped closer to the cabin. His chest seared in pain.

He didn't know what was happening, but he wasn't hanging around to find out.

He ran for his truck and jumped inside. Saxton jerked his shirt up and discovered his mark was a fiery, blood red.

His heartbeat pounded a deafening thump in his ears. His inner voice yelled, "Saxton, get the hell outta there, now!"

He quickly put the truck in gear, made a wide U-turn, and headed to his cabin on the other side of the park.

As the truck distanced itself from the girl's cabin, the burning ceased, and his heartbeat slowed.

He rounded the corner to his cabin, stopped, and threw the vehicle into park. He hurried to his door, fumbling with his keys as he ran.

Once inside, Saxton sprinted into the bathroom and ripped his shirt over his head.

He stared at his mark, still the hue of fresh blood. He watched as the mark pulsated with each heartbeat.

It seemed to take on a life of its own, over which he had no control.

Even though he was exhausted from burrowing through Geo's volumes of books, he knew sleep would not come easily that early morning.

Licah turned over and groaned. Her chest had been killing her off and on for about ten minutes.

The pain had finally subsided, but her heart still jackhammered in her chest.

She rolled out of bed and padded over to the bathroom.

She flipped on the light and squinted at the glare.

It took a moment for her vision to clear, but when it did, she gasped in shock.

At the collar of her chemise, she saw the top of her mark, and it was an angry red.

She pulled the neckline down and saw that the whole thing looked as fresh as the day it had mysteriously appeared all those years ago.

Suddenly the cool cabin was much too stuffy. She walked into the living room and onto the front porch hoping the fresh air would calm her.

A rocker that had seen better days was next to the door, and she tentatively sat down, hoping it wouldn't fall.

Once she was satisfied that she wasn't going to plunge to the deck, she leaned back and looked out over the park.

She could see taillights in the distance, heading toward the west end.

She figured it was the park ranger. The smoking girl had said that they would have the park to themselves.

She watched as lights flicked on in his cabin and wondered if he was having a rough night, too.

Then something popped into her head.

Two strangers, a world apart,
Standing idle with beating hearts,
Would that their space slowly close,
To feel the completeness a friendship
holds.

She knew she was being melodramatic, but she hadn't thought of anything creative in so long, she jumped from the rocker to write it down.

Hope filled her heart as she scribbled the words out on a napkin on the kitchen counter.

She looked at the twenty-three words with pride.

Maybe this trip was going to be worth the trouble.

Saxton poured a cup of coffee from the freshly brewed pot and walked over to Sam's desk.

She had the day off, and she usually left messages for him if something needed to be done.

He picked up a post-it note and read it.

Don't forget that Licah Daciana is renting the far eastern cabin, so don't run around the park naked... at least until I come back ;).

Sam

His heart tripped overtime, and he dropped into Sam's rolling chair.

He knew that name.

He had thought of that name every day for over a decade.

Licah Daciana

The girl with the emerald eyes.

The girl he had dreamt about.

The girl that had started it all.

He reached into the top drawer of Sam's desk and pulled out a steno notebook. It listed the phone numbers of each individual cabin. He traced his finger down one column and found Cabin 8.

His shaking hand reached for the phone, and he clumsily dialed the number.

One ring.

Two rings.

"Hello?"

That voice. He knew that voice like he knew his own skin.

"Hello? Is anyone there?"

Saxton took a deep breath and took the plunge.

"Hi, this is Ranger Lyall. I just wanted to check up on you this morning to see if your cabin was in order."

He was impressed with how steady his voice sounded.

He heard her typing away before she said, "Everything's fine. Thank you for calling."

He didn't want to hang up just yet. He yearned to hear more of her voice.

"Is there anything you need?" he asked, with a slight breathless quality to his voice.

She paused in her typing and asked, "What did you say your name was?"

"Ranger Lyall," he said softly, "Saxton Lyall."

The silence on the other end of the line was tangible.

Saxton felt the muscles in his throat begin to constrict.

Licah stared at the laptop screen, seeing through the text in front of her. Instead she saw her reflection and just a teasing of the mark, appearing just above her chemise.

"Saxton, I...," was all she could muster from her lips.

"Licah, it is so good to hear your voice after all these years," he bit his lip at the fear of saying too much.

After another brief silence, "It's good to hear yours, too. It's been a long time, hasn't it?"

Saxton swallowed hard. The inkling of a tear formed in the corner of his eye. "Almost nineteen years, but who's counting?"

Licah chuckled at his attempt to humor her. She had become accustomed to people remembering her for her novels, but not her as a person.

Saxton cleared his throat, the muscles starting to relax at her laughter.

"Licah, I figure you came down here to get away and be alone, but if it's not too much of an inconvenience, would you mind having supper with me tonight?" His heart seemed to stop at her silence.

Licah was at a loss for words. Her mind turned like the gears in a Swiss clock.

Before she could stop herself, she uttered, "Yes, it would be great to see you again."

Saxton nearly jumped in time with his racing heart. The grin on his face was wide enough a clown would have commended him.

Almost in time with Licah's words, Sam strolled into the lobby, the bittersweet smell of her cigarette still lingering about her.

Sam looked at Saxton and noticed the toothy smile on his lips. He flashed her an odd look, knowing she was off work that day.

She started to speak, but she could tell that she had interrupted something important. Whatever the conversation, she deduced it was most likely none of her business.

The grin quickly faded from Saxton's face. He looked Sam dead in the eyes and blushed, all of his blood pumping to his head.

He cleared his throat again and said, "Okay great! If you like, why not meet me at my cabin at eight o'clock, and I'll have supper made for you?"

"That would be nice, Saxton. I'm looking forward to us getting a chance to talk. We never really did in high school," her pulse speeding up double time.

Saxton motioned to Sam to take her seat, the phone propped on his right shoulder, "Okay. I'll see you at eight o'clock. My cabin is on the opposite end of the park from you. There will be a white Ford truck parked in front of it. It'll be great to talk with you, too. You have a good day and if there is anything you need, please call the office. Sam or I will get you taken care of."

Sam looked at Saxton with a bit of jealously shining in her eyes. "Thanks, boss," she whispered mockingly.

Licah thanked him, and Saxton heard the line disconnect. He sat the receiver down on its cradle and looked at Sam. The look on her face was not one of her usual perky expressions.

"So, got a date tonight, I see?" The sarcasm was thicker than the smoke rings she usually puffed on the office's front porch.

Saxton tried to be polite.

"Yeah, she's an old friend from high school. I have not laid eyes on her since my senior year. She moved away without even saying a word to anyone. I always wondered why she left."

Sam frowned, "Had a crush on her, did ya?"

Saxton backed into his office door, stuttering as he spoke, "What? No, it's nothing like that. Just thought it would be good to see how she has been after all these years."

With an indifferent shrug, Sam turned away from Saxton.

He quickly closed his office door, leaving a scowling Sam behind.

He thought to himself, "Man, she is pissed!"

He walked over to his desk, sliding into his chair.

He looked out the window at the leaves falling from the trees as the autumn wind picked up.

After a long deep breath mixed with anticipation of that night and uneasiness where Sam was concerned, Saxton wished he had a good strong cup of coffee from McGuire's.

He thought of asking Sam to fetch him one, but knew that was not the best idea.

The way she was fuming, she might put bug spray in it.

Licah looked at the phone sitting in the cradle by the refrigerator and didn't know what to think.

After all these years of not seeing Saxton, her mark had been dormant. Now, after a night of the mark burning like it had when she was a teenager, he turns out to be the park ranger.

This was no coincidence.

Jessica had told her years ago that Saxton bore the same mark she did.

She wondered if he still had his.

She started to pick the phone back up and realized she didn't know the number.

Maybe she should pay a little visit to the office to see if her mark burned again at his nearness.

Then she thought of the smoking secretary and thought better of it.

She would take the day and stock the cabin. Afterward, she would put on her best outfit and go see what fate had in store for her.

Chapter Five

Licah put up the last of the groceries and glanced at the clock.

It was already three in the afternoon.

She had thrown herself into her writing after her phone conversation with Saxton to get away from her thoughts.

She now had twenty pages of a horror novel that she had no idea how she had ended up writing.

She had never been into horror. She had always tried to write books that were informative with an interesting twist.

Jo was going to freak out when she saw the pages she had written.

Rutland, Cochran, and Pennington wasn't a horror publisher, but she was almost positive her friend would publish anything she put her name to.

She sat back down on the barstool where she had been perched when Saxton had called that morning, and slid her finger over the touchpad on her laptop.

The book seemed to have taken a mind of its own that morning.

The small bit of prose she had scribbled out the night before was on the first page, centered and italicized.

It had all started with watching Saxton's brake lights.

He obviously wasn't married, or he would have mentioned his wife being there for dinner. Right?

Uncertainty rushed through her for a moment, and then she shook her head to clear it.

He would have said something.

He had seemed so nervous on the phone with her. Maybe his mark had burned, too.

She set her cell phone alarm to go off, at seven-thirty and threw herself into her writing again.

She was on page seventy-five when her alarm went off and she looked up only to find she had a crick in her neck from being bent over her laptop for so long.

Her rear end was numb as she got off the barstool and walked back to the master bedroom.

She reached into the closet and took out a slinky long-sleeved green dress her mother had bought her for book signings.

"It is the exact same color as your eyes. I knew you had to have it," her mother had said when she had given it to her.

She slipped the dress on and brushed her hair until it shone.

Her makeup was hurriedly, but stylishly done, and she checked to make sure the dress covered the mark.

She could just see the top edge of the claws, and she made a mental note to check it throughout the night to make sure it stayed mostly hidden.

She looked in the mirror again and shrugged.

"Now or never," she said, grabbing her purse and walking out the door.

Saxton paced around the table, checking all the details on its oval shaped oak surface.

His white apron was somewhat twisted to his right side as he made his orbit around.

He had straightened the napkins and silverware a score of times. His fine kitchenware was neatly centered in front of each seat.

It had been a long time since Saxton had prepared a meal for anyone, other than his mom.

It wasn't something he felt comfortable doing. His meals usually came out of a can or a dish that had taken a three-minute spin in the microwave.

Saxton's dining room was sparsely lit. Two candles sat on the table an arm's length from one another.

He pulled a box of matches from one of the kitchen drawers.

The smell of the lit match took him back to a day of roasting marshmallows on a shaved stick and talking about girls at summer campouts with his friends.

The room seemed to glow with his excitement of seeing Licah again.

He didn't really even know her. But he fondly remembered the time she had laid her silky, petite hand on his shoulder to comfort him at the school dance.

Saxton walked over to the CD player and punched up a Tony Bennett song, and lowered the volume to a whisper.

He almost blushed at his actions.

"She is going to think I'm trying to get her in the sack."

His head turned in the direction of his bedroom, and he grinned with mirth.

"At least I washed the sheets this week," he said to himself in a sarcastic tone.

He had no plans of such events. However, he did remember how beautiful she had been in school.

He recalled how everyone called her the gypsy girl and that just added to her mystery. But lastly, he recalled how she had disappeared from Parker's Ridge without as much as a word.

Saxton remembered Jessica's admission to him that Licah had the same mark as the one on his chest.

He remembered what Geo had told him it meant. If the information was correct, Licah was Saxton's soul mate, and he longed for the sight of her again.

He dreamed of the feel of her soft lips against his. He lusted for the smell of her soft skin and the texture of her lovely mane brushing across his cheek.

However, although his mind played out the events perfectly, his knowledge of the curse also filled him with fear.

The timer on the stove brought him back to life.

He darted to the oven and took out the one fine dish he knew how to make well, crab stuffed mushrooms.

The aroma filled the kitchen and carried throughout his cabin.

Saxton walked to the table and placed the mushrooms, one by one, onto the awaiting plates. He placed the empty Pyrex pan in the sink, the smoke still rolling from its surface.

Reaching over to the kitchen counter, Saxton picked up a bowel of fresh salad. The small, red tomatoes reflecting the candle light as he placed the bowl on the table.

Pacing backward, he looked at his creation. Then it dawned on him, "Drinks!"

He ran to the refrigerator and pulled out a longed-neck bottle of Etude Pinot Gris.

He walked to the sink and unfastened the end of the bottle. Grabbing a corkscrew from the drawer, he twisted and yanked out the cork with an impressive pop.

The smell of chilled lemon followed by faint pear and honeysuckle filled his nostrils.

Taking two glasses from the kitchen's bar area, he placed them on the table and poured the liquid into each clear container until the bubbles almost erupted from the rim.

He placed the cork back in the bottle and sat it back in the refrigerator.

Saxton stepped away one more time and surveyed the scene, "Perfect!"

He then untied his apron and hurriedly put it in one of the kitchen drawers.

Charging into the bathroom, he went to make sure he was in tip-top condition.

He smiled at his reflection in the mirror, trying to hide his nervousness from himself.

This first impression had to count when it concerned Licah. It may never come again.

As he gave himself the once-over, he felt the strange burn in his chest, "Dear Lord, not now...please!"

With a groan he doubled over in the floor, his chest feeling as though a thousand knifes had plunged into his heart.

Saxton crawled out of the bathroom and toward the dining room when a knock came at the door.

He rolled into the stereo and caused the CD to skip and lock up on its beautiful lyrics.

He screamed in pain as his teeth stretched in his mouth. His nose became elongated, and his ears began to point.

Ginger-red hair started shooting from every follicle of his body until his clothes bulged from lack of space.

He looked down at the fur that spread across his fair complexion.

He could feel his back leg muscles twist and pulsate in agony.

He tried to pull himself up on the dining room table, but only managed to knock his lovingly made meal on the floor with him.

His clothes ripped away from his body as his torso grew in size.

The sound of the pounding at the door grew louder and more labored. He could hear a girl whimpering in pain just outside.

The door burst open to reveal Licah, painfully gripping her heart. Her feet caught on the threshold, and she landed undignified in the floor.

The agony coursing through Licah's body was suddenly pushed to the side at the sight before her.

She lay on the floor as still as she could and looked at the monstrous beast only a few feet away.

The creature lay face up, its breathing labored and harsh through its nostrils. It was much larger than a man; red fur covered its entire body, which was ripped with muscle.

She realized she had been holding her breath and sucked air in like she had never breathed before.

Its head rotated to face her, and she looked dead into a pair of very human gray eyes.

The beast's nose and ears were like that of a wolf, and the teeth showing above that lolling tongue looked sharp as daggers.

She stayed perfectly still as it rolled to its stomach and turned toward her. She could see a spot bare of hair on the wolf creature's chest.

A mark.

Just like her own.

Her gaze went back to those gray eyes, and she felt a calmness fall over her. Her chest didn't hurt anymore, but the beast had different ideas.

It snarled at her and ran across the living room. The creature crashed through the front picture window, and disappeared into the night.

As soon as her heart stopped pounding, she picked herself up from the floor and glanced out the window.

She couldn't see anything, but the moonlit park.

She woodenly walked over to the table and lovingly picked up the broken dishes and remains of a meal that had obviously taken Saxton hours to prepare.

She looked up in shock, and then sat heavily in one of the ladder back chairs.

She felt her heart drop from her chest.

Saxton was a werewolf.

Saxton had a mark like her own.

Saxton had always run away from her.

Was she the cause?

The trip back to her cabin was the work of only a few minutes with her strong legs, and she nearly tripped in her heels as she raced for the phone.

She picked it up and dialed her mother.

"Da?" she heard her mother grunt.

Normally Licah would have apologized for waking her up, but she had a burning need to know the meaning of this.

"Mother, why did you send me away from Parker's Ridge when I was a teenager?" she asked hurried, kicking her shoes off and plopping down on the barstool.

"Ce sa întâmplat?" her mother asked "What happened?" in Romanian.

This was a problem that she had never been able to break her mother of. She always reverted back to her native tongue when she was tired or upset.

"English, Mother!" she yelled probably louder than she should have.

She heard her mother clear her throat, "What has happened, Licah?"

Licah shook her head and walked over to the couch and collapsed into it.

"No, you tell me here and now, why did you send me away?"

"When the mark showed up on you, it was the only thing your bunicâ and I could do."

Licah felt as if her breath had been knocked from her chest.

They had known about the mark. There had been more to it than just coincidence. And they had never told her.

Saxton was out there suffering because she had come back to Parker's Ridge, and her mother and grandmother had known all along what would have happened if they were to meet again.

"Tell me everything, or so help me, you will never see me again."

Rage, hate, guilt, fear, loneliness.

That was all that Saxton knew as he ran through the park's one hundred acre landscape.

He was moving at such a high rate of speed, he could not make out a single detail of his surroundings.

There was no thought, no plan, just *run*. Keep running as fast as he could.

Saxton's hot breath steamed the night air. He could occasionally make out the top of a paw where his hand used to be.

Run, run, run.

That's all Saxton knew.

Trees whizzed by like boards on a picket fence as he darted here and there among the trees.

Saxton had no idea where he was or where he was going.

Run, run, run.

His vision never locked onto any single object, other than to dodge whatever was in his way.

His soul was on fire. His emotions felt like stones being whirled at him by a thousand invisible hands.

Run, run, run.

He could see a light in the distance. It was a cabin, the illumination pouring from a large rectangular hole.

Saxton's pace slowed, his breath heavy. He approached the light as if stalking an animal for the kill.

Saxton's head peered out from the bottom of a large cedar tree. The building looked familiar to a part of him, but his werewolf instincts told him to treat it with extreme caution.

Saxton's breath had returned to normal, and he padded his way to the cabin.

A large hole was all that remained of a picture window on the building.

He snarled at the shards of glass sinking into his tender paws.

Unknowingly to Saxton, he had been traveling around the park in circles, and he had returned to the place from whence he came.

He did not know this was his home, however. The werewolf part of his mind had blurred most of his memory.

At the sight of the table through the fractured hole, the image of a beautiful woman strained to come into his thoughts.

He stressed to recall her name, but her face was all he could remember from the time before his eerie transformation.

Licah was her name. *Sweet Licah*, where had she gone?

Saxton crawled on the concrete slab at the base of the back porch and laid on his stomach and chest. The cold stone felt good against the mark on his torso.

Closing his eyes, he laid his muzzle on his paws, still felt the energy of his emotions lingering throughout his body.

As he lay still, his mind cleared, and his body released its tension. The waves of red fur slowly dissipated, and his features returned to normal.

Saxton lay on the concrete, completely naked. His limbs were drawn against his frame, and he was falling fast asleep.

Licah walked tentatively up to the park office, squinting in the sunlight, and waited to feel the searing pain of the night before.

She had to talk to Saxton. Had to make sure he was okay.

She opened the office door without a hint of a burn and saw Sam, the smoking girl, sitting in the office chair.

The venom in her gaze worried Licah as she walked up to the desk.

"Is Ranger Lyall here?" she asked, trying not to fidget.

The girl leaned back in her chair and crossed her arms over her voluptuous chest.

"What was your name again?" she asked huffily.

It must have been hard keeping up with the one renter in the park.

"I'm Licah Daciana. I need to speak with him."

The girl looked at her strangely for several moments, then flipped open a date book.

"Oh, I'm sorry, it seems that Ranger Lyall has gone on vacation and won't be back for at least a week. Ranger Johnson will be here tomorrow to fill his post. If you can wait until then, I'll have Greg call you."

Licah did well in hiding her expression.

He was on vacation?

How could he leave her hanging like this?

"That won't be necessary," she answered, turning around and walking back out the door.

She didn't bother to say goodbye. It was quite obvious the girl didn't care.

The following afternoon, Saxton white-knuckled the steering wheel of the white Ford, as he drove north on the interstate.

The events of the past few days dug through his mind like a mole.

He had known seeing Licah would probably have some adverse effects, but nothing like what had happened.

He traveled up the mountainous highway, taking the occasional half glance at his sleeping companion.

He replayed his visit with Geo that had taken place just before departing on his current journey.

Saxton had stood in front of Geo's desk, his eyes red from lack of sleep.

He explained the events of his supper with Licah as Geo listened intently to every sound and syllable.

Geo's face was filled with concern as the story unfolded.

Saxton informed him the first thing he remembered was awakening completely naked at his own front door.

Once Saxton finished, he looked at Geo with a strong feeling of fear, "What am I going to do?"

Geo paused as he mulled over his answer, "I think you need to take a trip to Maine and see what you can unearth about this old book." Geo held the book in his hand while drumming his fingers on it a few times.

Saxton spoke through clenched teeth, "Is that the book that explains this damned curse?"

Geo nodded and handed it to him, "You still have the other books you borrowed from me?"

Saxton accepted the book and replied, "Yes, I got three books from you the other night, and they are still in my truck seat."

"Good, then you have no need to go back to the park," Geo said, deadpan.

"But what about…"

Geo interrupted, "No! Do not go back to the park. If you see or even get near Licah, you will change. We really aren't sure what you are capable of in that state."

Saxton agreed. No need to put Licah, or Sam for that matter, in danger, "I understand. So where in Maine am I going?"

Geo shook his head, "Not you. Both of us. I'm coming too. You have no idea what questions to ask or where exactly to look."

Saxton's brow tightened, "So I guess you know how to do those things?"

"Son, listen. You have about a snowball's chance in hell of figuring this out on your own, and for your sake and the sake of Licah, I should go with you."

Saxton had repeated his earlier question, "So where in Maine are we going?"

"Bangor. It's the site of one of the earliest settlements in Maine."

Saxton's mind returned to the open road and his passenger propped up beside him.

134

Geo began to softly snore, and the truck levelly traveled up the lonely Tennessee landscape.

"I hope you know what you're doing, Geo," Saxton thought out loud.

Chapter Six

Licah fumbled with the radio in her Wrangler as she headed through Parker's Ridge.

She just needed a quick change of scenery. All the events from the night before and that morning had clogged her mind and she needed some time away from the park.

Licah pulled her jeep into the town's only gas station and got out to get a bottle of water. However, she really felt the need for something a lot stronger.

She strolled inside and there stood Jackson, behind the counter.

He smiled at her in a way that flirted with danger.

She didn't mind. He wasn't too hard on the eyes, other than the greasy hands and the black smudge under his chin.

Jack's eyes sparkled as he spoke, "Well hello, Ms. Licah. How has your stay been so far? Already bored with the small town life, huh?"

Licah rolled her eyes, "Not at all. It has actually been very interesting to be back in Parker's Ridge."

Jack took off his hat and placed it on the counter.

His long black hair fell over his ears, "The more things change, the more they stay the same, right?"

Licah smiled politely and nodded, "Yes, I would have to agree."

With that, she turned and went to the drink cooler to find water.

Jack marched from behind the counter and headed in her direction.

She half smiled at his approach. His intent was pretty see-through.

He walked to her side, his rag rolled into a ball in his greasy hands, "Um, Licah? I was wondering, since it has been so long since you have been to town, I wondered if I could take you out sometime this week? There is a new restaurant here in Parker's Ridge, and I hear the food is very good."

Licah almost laughed out loud at his southern pleasantries.

She didn't really know how to respond.

She just stared into the cooler, pretending to look for bottled water.

After a several seconds of silence, Jack offered, "Tell you what, I will make this easy for you. I will give you my card, and you can mull the idea over."

Jack returned to the counter and picked up a card from a small stack.

Licah quickly grabbed water from the cooler door and walked up to pay for it.

She placed it next to the register and looked at Jack, her cheeks burning from embarrassment.

It wasn't that she didn't like Jack, but her mind was far from dating.

Jack handed her his card and smiled, "Just think it over."

Licah took the card and placed it in her pocket with a smile. She fished out a couple of dollars to pay for the water and stretched out her hand to give him the money.

Jack waved at her and said, "It's on me."

Licah really didn't know what to say but, "Thank you," finally came from her lips.

Jack placed his hat back on his head, "You are very welcome, Ms. Licah, and I hope to hear from you soon."

Licah strode out of the gas station door and got into her jeep.

The whole situation was a bit awkward for her, but she wasn't offended.

Jack and his attentions were a refreshing change from the normal New York charm, but he couldn't have picked a worse time.

Licah started the engine and pulled out of the parking lot, "He is nice," she finally admitted, trying to convince herself that everything was normal.

Saxton sat shotgun in his truck, with Geo at the wheel. He held the four books that belonged to his driving companion on his right knee.

Geo had volunteered to drive and Saxton had gratefully accepted.

He had been so sleepy, not just from this trip to Maine, but from the horrible episode the night before.

The few hours of rest had been just enough to satisfy his bodies sleep allowance.

He knew when they returned to Tennessee, he would probably sleep for a good twenty-four hours straight.

His thoughts went to Licah and the date that had almost been.

He missed getting to see her and feared he may never get the chance again.

To clear his mind of such thoughts, Saxton looked at the printout that had been lying on the dash.

It was a fifteen hundred mile one-way trip to Bangor. If they drove nonstop, they could get there in about twenty-four hours. Between him and Geo, they had covered at least half that distance.

Saxton yawned as he turned to Geo, "Where are we?"

Geo yawned in return, "Somewhere in Virginia. If we continue to swap up driving, we should be there by tomorrow afternoon."

Saxton picked up one of the books and sat the others in the floorboard.

He cracked open the one titled *"Romanian Genealogy, 1720-1760."* The pages were old and brittle.

He flipped on the passenger side reading light and maneuvered through its pages.

The tome was filled with columns and columns of last names.

He squinted to read the faded text and ran his finger down the alphabetical list.

He first went to the L's and turned the page over to continue the listing.

His finger stopped, and he gasped when he saw his own name, Lyall.

He thrust the book at Geo in excited thoughtlessness, "Look at this!"

Geo swerved on the interstate, nearly running the truck into the side of a passing trailer truck, "Calm down!" He straightened the truck back into his lane, "What is it?!"

Saxton pulled the book away from the front of Geo's face, "It lists my family name in this Romanian genealogy book. I had no clue my father's ancestors were from Romania. I always thought his family was from Ireland."

Saxton noted the page number the index referenced and gently flipped the age-dried pages till he found the one that had the name Lyall in bold text.

There was very little mentioned of his family, other than the names of three brothers and a sister.

The eldest son was simply listed as D. Lyall and told of his marrying a woman in Dublin, Ireland, whose name was not known.

The marriage was thought to have taken place around the year 1744, and they had had one son, named William Riley Lyall. After that, there was no other mention of the Lyall family.

Saxton relayed all this information to Geo, his voice loaded with intrigue.

Geo listened intensively to the family's origin, "Well, this would explain why you thought your family was from Ireland. It sounds as though your direct descendant moved away from Romania and went to live there."

Saxton shrugged as he thumbed through the book again, "It would appear so, but there is no mention of his younger brother's and sister's family."

Geo's mind clicked forward, "Check to see if Licah's family name is listed."

Saxton turned back to the index, the book about to fall apart from over use. He came to the D's and looked until he found the last name, Daciana.

Finding the listing for the page number to be '185', he turned eagerly.

Maybe this would tell him something about the beautiful gypsy girl of which he knew so little.

Saxton arrived at page '184' and looked to the following page which had '187' printed on its old parchment. He ran his fingers down the inside of the book's spine to find a little jagged line of paper.

In disgust, he dropped the book, which closed with a dusty clunk, onto his lap, "The damn page is missing! Just like in this other book." Saxton pointed to one of the other volumes at his feet, "Who has been ripping pages out of these books?"

Geo mulled over his question just as the very first rays of sunlight began to make their way from the east, "I'm not sure son, but whatever is going on, it has been known about by certain people for a long time, and they are taking measures to see that it stays a secret."

A feeling of dread cascaded down Saxton's body. This curse he had been tossed into was starting to sound more and more sinister than just merely turning into a werewolf.

There was a cause for this entire charade, and he feared he would not like the answer.

Licah lay in bed watching the sun ascend the horizon.

Saxton still hadn't returned to his cabin.

She had spent the day at the market getting the basics for a few weeks and then at the cabin getting everything arranged to her liking. All the while she peered out the window to see if Saxton's truck had returned.

She hadn't been able to write another word without thinking about the conversation she'd had with her mother.

Apparently when Licah let her mother see the mark, she'd panicked. She told her that they moved to Parker's Ridge to get away from so many men that might be Licah's possible soul mate.

Soul mate.

Saxton was her soul mate.

How did she know this?

According to her mother, every Daciana woman was cursed to find their soul mate. Once their eyes met, a mark showed up over their hearts to mark them as each other's.

Then, horrifyingly enough, the male would turn into a werewolf.

If she hadn't seen it with her own eyes, she would have driven to Virginia to put her mother in a mental hospital.

But she had been right.

Licah talked to her for over an hour, her grandmother speaking Romanian close at hand.

Apparently her mother, grandmother, great grandmother, and all her previous female relatives had gone through the same thing.

One of her great grandmothers times seven or eight, Yeaserna Daciana, had cursed the man she loved, Dak Lyall, because he'd married another woman.

In grief and heartache, she'd cursed her descendants to a life of horror and sorrow.

When a Daciana woman met her soul mate, destined to be a descendant of Yeaserna's cursed lover, he turned into a werewolf. It was then her job to ensure that the amulet, which Licah had in her witch's bag, was placed around her mate's neck by her own hand.

All had survived. But some, only just.

When Licah asked what the amulet did, her mother explained that as long as her mate wore the amulet, he wouldn't turn.

It didn't take her long to ask why there was only one.

The Daciana women couldn't possibly have shared one amulet.

When she inquired, her grandmother requested the phone.

"Draga mea dragoste," she had begun, calling her "my dearest love", "each Daciana makes a pact when they meet their mate, that they will pass on the amulet once the next generation meets theirs. When your mother met your father, your grandfather turned the amulet over to her and moved away to parts unknown."

Licah was shocked.

She always thought her grandfather had died in a car accident.

She explained that he still called her on their anniversary, but otherwise didn't speak. She said it was just too hard.

Her mother knew this and quickly informed her that her father had indeed died of cancer, but she had held the amulet in case the curse ever passed on to Licah.

She had hoped to circumvent the curse by moving to a little Podunk town in Tennessee.

It had to be a billion to one chance that a descendant of Dak Lyall would be living in the same country town as she. Licah pondered those odds till her head began to ache. Before hanging up the phone, she had taken an ibuprofen and wished them well.

Now, as she not so patiently awaited Saxton's return, she wasn't sure what to do.

She didn't know his phone number.

She was sure that Miss Lung Cancer wasn't going to give it to her.

She closed her laptop and sighed.

It was a good thing that Jo had given her three months, at this rate, she wasn't going to have anything written other than what she had written that first day in the cabin.

Saxton was back behind the wheel of his Ford truck. The naps he had taken throughout the trip to Maine had lost their effectiveness.

The only thing that seemed to help was the cold air pouring in from the open driver's side window. The chilled air relaxed his thoughts but also kept his drooping eyelids open.

Saxton looked over at Geo, who was snoring softly again. He had wadded his coat tightly under his head as a makeshift pillow and was catching up on some much needed sleep.

The sun was starting its slow decent into the west when Saxton saw a sign reading *Bangor 15 miles*.

He sighed at seeing it. He knew he would have to poke Geo soon to figure out exactly where they were going.

Saxton reached over with his right hand and gave Geo a light nudge. His eyes opened, and he robotically turned his head.

"We're nearly there, Geo. What part of Bangor are we heading to?"

Geo pulled out a map, and pointed to a spot that had been circled with a red marker.

Saxton slightly turned his head so that he could see the interstate as well as the map, "That looks like the middle of nowhere to me."

"In a way, it is. Not much in that part of the city anymore, other than an old sawmill and maybe an old church."

Geo continued with his instructions, his hands moving as if tracing a snake's back. Apparently, this was not a 'straight-to-it' trip to Bangor.

Once he finished speaking, he put his hand on Saxton's shoulder, "Son, I'm not real sure what, if anything, we are gonna find up here. This is a one in a million shot."

Saxton groaned at Geo's words. They had driven fifteen hundred miles for a one in a million shot? What was Geo thinking?

As they passed an exit sign on the interstate, Geo pointed to the upcoming off ramp, "Can we pull off here? I need something to eat."

Saxton was hungry too. Neither one of them had eaten very much on the pilgrimage north.

He moved the car toward the right and merged into the ramp lane.

He pulled into a lonely mom-'n-pop restaurant just off the busy interstate.

He found the closest parking spot to the door and turned off the truck.

Geo stepped out and stretched his short legs to the ground, "I ain't made for long trips no more." Saxton could hear his back cracking as he stretched.

Geo turned and looked at Saxton, "Son, you coming in?"

Saxton scratched the top of his red hair, "Yeah, I'll be inside in a minute. I need to make a phone call."

Geo grinned a knowing smile and headed into the restaurant.

Once Geo was out of sight, Saxton took his cell phone from his pocket.

He thumbed through the address book and found the number labeled *'Park Office'*. He pushed the button to call, and a voice almost immediately answered the phone. "Sam must be bored," he thought out loud.

Sam's young voice echoed in his ear, "Thank you for calling Stone Creek Park Office. How can I help you today?"

"Sam, this is Saxton. I need you to..."

"Saxton! Where the hell did you go? You left without a word. Just a stupid note that said you were going on vacation! Vacation?! You never go anywhere! And that guy, Ranger Johnson, he's the biggest idiot I have…"

"Look Sam, I don't have time to explain. I need you to connect me to Licah's cabin. I need to talk to her."

Saxton could hear Sam's blood boiling on the other end of the phone, "Oh! I see how it is. You call up here to talk to your new girlfriend! I have a good mind to turn this squirrel I caught in my attic loose in her cabin and see how that city slicker…"

Saxton yelled into his cell phone. His voice being louder than he had heard it in years, "I don't have time to listen to your jealous gobble-de-gook! Now connect me to the damn cabin!"

Saxton could hear the young girl mumbling something under her breath about 'damn yankees' when he heard the connection change over and begin to ring.

It rang once and again, "Hello?" Licah's voice was filled with worry.

Saxton froze for a minute and then spoke softly, "Licah, it's me, Saxton."

Licah's breath caught in her throat as she stood at the kitchen counter.

She hadn't known if he had really left or if the smoking girl just told her that to throw her off the scent.

She took a deep breath and said, "Hi."

Saxton closed his eyes and tried to focus on her breathing.

The mark on his chest tingled at the thought of her.

"Are you okay?" he asked softly, hoping the answer was yes. The fact that she hadn't hung up on him gave him hope.

She sat there for a moment and thought about his question.

"No. I'm not okay," she replied.

He took a deep breath to apologize when she began again.

"I'm really worried about you and pissed off that you took off without talking to me about what happened. I have things I need to tell you. Important things."

Saxton chuckled. He'd take a tongue-lashing any day to freaking out or crying.

"What's so funny?" she asked indignantly.

He chuckled again.

"You're not screaming in terror or hanging up on me. I find that very funny."

She paused and started to chuckle herself.

"You're right. I'm not. But you knew I was weird the day you met me."

He nodded and realized she couldn't see it.

"I'm in Maine. I'm trying to find out information on this... problem," he said, not wanting to say werewolf curse out loud.

"Well, I need you here. I have the solution," she fired back.

His eyes popped open.

"What do you mean you have the solution?"

Licah sighed.

"Saxton, please come home."

Saxton's breathe caught in his lungs.

Home.

She wanted him to come home.

"I can't, sweetie. I've got to figure this out. I'm with Geo, and we're trying to track down a friend of his who might know more about this."

Licah felt her temper flare.

"That's what I'm trying to tell you. I already know about it. It's my fault this happened to you."

Tears streamed down Licah's cheeks, and she suddenly couldn't breathe.

"Licah? It's not your fault, okay?"

"It is. It's a curse that was laid on my family centuries ago. It happened to my dad and my grandfather and who knows who else."

Saxton sat up and took notice.

"Are they still alive?"

Right after he asked it, he knew he shouldn't have. She was already upset.

"My grandfather is, but my dad died of cancer a long time ago."

He was surprised how matter-of-factly she said it.

"Were you not close to them?" he asked, wincing again.

Licah sighed and sniffled.

"I never knew either of them. I didn't even know my grandfather was still alive until my grandmother told me when I asked about the *Blestemul Vârcolac de Dragoste*."

Saxton shook his head. She even knew what it was called.

"Listen, I've got to go; Geo's waiting for me. Write this number down," he gave her his cell phone number, "I'll call you tonight after we meet with his friend, and you can tell me all about it."

"Saxton, I have the amulet. I don't know if you know about it, but if I can get it around your neck while you're a wolf, you won't change anymore as long as you wear it."

Licah reached into her pocket and fingered the old amulet.

It was made of bronze and had a large paw print in the center that looked exactly like the mark over her heart. Around the outer circle, the words: *teamă de fiara în cadrul* were written in Romanian. Fear the beast within.

"Geo had told me there was once a cure, I guess that's it," he responded with hope in his voice.

His heart resounded with relief. That was one less thing they had to worry about, finding the cure. Licah already had it.

Then he thought about what she had said.

"What do you mean you have to put it around my neck while I'm a wolf?" he asked harshly. "I'm not putting you in that kind of danger!"

Licah's spine stiffened as she leaned over the counter and spoke calmly, but commandingly through the phone.

"Listen to me. You are in this mess because of me. I will do whatever I have to to get you out of it."

Her words calmed him, somewhat, but he still didn't want to wolf out near her.

They had both been lucky last time. He wasn't going to take that chance again, even if it meant not getting near her for the rest of his life.

"I'll call you later, okay?"

Licah stood back up and said, "Okay."

Chapter Seven

Saxton and Geo stood on a hillside overlooking what used to be a thriving city a few hundred years ago. The cold air ruffled through Saxton's ginger hair; and Geo sank his hands deeper into his pockets.

After much contemplation, Saxton had decided against telling Geo of Licah's phone call.

They had driven for over a day to get to Bangor. There didn't seem to be any reason not to look around the old part of town and see what clues could be put together on the devilish curse.

Not only that, but he could tell that Geo was playing on a hunch, or he would not have taken part in the trip.

Saxton assured himself it would be in everyone's best interests to see what Geo might turn up.

There was little that remained in thie old part of Bangor. The skeleton of an ancient sawmill could be seen at one end of the old township. An old church sat slowly turning to dust as the cold winds beat against its old whitewashed frame. There were also a half a dozen houses that looked to be occupied by actual living residents.

Leaving his truck on the top of the steep hill, Saxton shivered in the wind as they made their way down toward the time beaten road. His boots slipped slightly in the damp grass, "Where to now, Geo?"

Geo pointed in the direction of the old church, without speaking. It was almost as if he tasted the air to figure out his first move.

As they approached the church, Saxton could sense something about the place, something that unsettled him to his core.

Grabbing Geo by the arm, they stopped a few yards from the church's wide front stairs.

"Something's different here. I'm feeling...I don't know. I don't like it here."

Rubbing at the scar on his chest, his thoughts went to Licah. He prayed she was okay.

He already missed her terribly.

Saxton started for the church steps, and Geo followed behind.

Not saying a word, Geo studied Saxton's movement. He looked as if he were stalking up on the church, just like a wolf would do when confronting another animal not known to him.

Saxton pushed open one of the doors to the ancient house of worship, and ageless dust leaked from its hinges.

It was obvious no one had set foot in the place for years.

Geo broke his silence. "I need you to tell me anytime you feel anything strange. It could work to our advantage."

Saxton nodded, still looking forward.

As they walked into the church, the smell of musky air and rotting wood nearly over took them.

The wooden church benches were completely covered in a quarter-of-an-inch of fine dust. A few old hymnals lay in the main aisle leading to the altar.

They each looked down the rows as they passed, making sure there wasn't anything that needed their attention.

The two arrived at the front of the church, and they surveyed their surroundings.

The altar was nearly collapsing on itself.

A dove hummed by from a rafter, and escaped through a crack in one of the old stained glass windows.

Geo walked straight past the altar and behind the pulpit.

Stopping at the back right corner, he bent down and examined the dirt-covered walls.

He ran his hands up, pushing with each pass of his fingers. His hands stopped and a small grin lit up his face, "Ah ha!"

A small click echoed through the old choir loft as Geo slid a hidden panel away from its resting place.

White powdery dust filled his lungs, and he coughed to fight it away.

"What did you find?" Saxton asked as he approached behind Geo.

"This is what they used to call a priest hole. It was somewhere for the priest to hide out, if need be."

Geo removed a pocket-sized flashlight and motioned at Saxton, "I'm a bit too weak in the knees to get down into this. If you will check it out, I will hold the flashlight."

Saxton looked Geo straight in the eyes and nodded, "I hope you've got fresh batteries in that thing.

Saxton looked at the four-foot opening. A deep sense of dread cast over him.

Bending down, he went head first into the compartment. The beam from Geo's flashlight was having a hard time penetrating the years of spider webs and dirt that hung in his way.

He took his arm and wiped them from sight. The compartment was very small. There was just enough room for two people, if they were crouching down.

Saxton gazed into the dark, his pulse jumping with fear.

He examined the floor; and all he saw inside was blackness. Finding nothing of interest, he turned his vision to the sides of the room.

On the three walls facing him, Saxton could make out something in the wood construct.

He started to shake a bit, his tall body stressing from the awkward position. It appeared to be writing at first. But then he narrowed his eyes to help make out what it said.

It was not writing at all. It was claw marks, hundreds of them.

He fell back, his heart racing, "I gotta get out of here!"

Saxton crawled out in reverse. His back hung on the edge of the room's small opening. Breaking free, he nearly flattened Geo as he escaped.

"What did you see, son?" Geo requested.

"There are claw marks all over the walls! They must have locked someone in here once."

Geo frowned, "Not what I was hoping for." He stepped away from the pulpit area and headed to the first row of pews.

Saxton stood, still feeling the ever-present twinge at his chest, "I need you to level with me Geo. What did you expect to find up here?"

Geo turned back to face Saxton and frowned again. He thought for a moment and noticed Saxton began to slowly slump over.

He opened his mouth to speak when the church doors collided with the interior walls, the old, wooden frames disintegrating into splinters.

Geo took a defensive stance as he dug into his pocket.

There before him stood, on four enormous padded paws, a charcoal black living nightmare.

The beast's eyes were filled with rage. He could see saliva dripping from it's elongated canine teeth. The hairs on it's head bristled.

He could hear the monster-hound's breath the full length of the church away.

Without looking in his direction, he screamed, "Saxton, get in the priest hole! Now!"

There was no reply.

Geo stood at the center aisle, his old feet planted steadfastly on the wooden floor. A small container was held just under his index finger, aimed directly at the hairy beast.

"Descendant of Lyall, away from here!! I order you back to the place whence you came! You have been warned!" The sound of his own voice roared in his ears.

The beast took no notice of Geo.

With no warning, a red streak of lightning arched over Geo's head.

The ginger beast jumped the length of the church to land, claws extended, onto the black nightmare in front of him.

Geo's mind jumped into action as the two beasts bit and clawed for each other's throats.

Saliva rained everywhere inside the timeworn church.

The animals locked together and began to roll into the back row of old pews. Splinters shot across the room, some burying up in Geo's legs.

Jolting forward with the speed of a track runner, Geo took the small container in his hand and sprayed the black werewolf square in the face.

The creature howled in agony, it's paws retracting from the red werewolf's neck.

The black beast righted itself and dashed out one of the church's stained-glass windows.

It's howls echoed throughout the old township. Colorful shards rained down on the other wolf-creature as it lay on the floor, motionless.

Geo ran to the beast's side, trying to look for signs of life. He could see it's lungs filling with air and exhaling, it's breathing horribly labored.

He took one paw and tightly squeezed, "Dear God, please don't let Saxton die..."

Licah sat in a corner shaking, her heart pounding in her chest, more afraid than she'd ever been in her life.

She had been proofreading her writing when suddenly fear had consumed her mind, and the only way to calm herself was to cower in a corner.

163

The phone rang, and she sat for several moments before she crawled over to the counter to grab her cell phone.

"He... hello?"

"Are you okay?" her mother asked in perfectly spoken English.

"How did you know?" she asked, taking shallow breaths to still her beating heart.

"Your grandmother is in the corner of the dining room crying. She said they have found each other."

Licah's eyebrows crinkled.

"Who has found each other?"

She heard her mother sigh over the phone.

"Her wolf. And yours."

Licah's limbs trembled.

"You mean that Saxton has met grandfather?" she asked in fright.

"Da. It also means that they are probably fighting to the death at this very moment. Two wolves of this nature cannot occupy the same territory and not attack each other for dominance. I haven't seen father since mother gave me the amulet."

Anca stopped for a moment and sighed.

"It was the only time I'd ever seen him. She told me not to try to find him because if he and your father met, they would have killed each other."

Geo leaned over Saxton, listening to his breathing as he laid on one of the abandoned church pews.

The young man had returned to his human form within minutes of the fight with the black werewolf.

Saxton was too heavy, and Geo too worn from the long trip to carry him to the truck on the top of the hill.

Instead, he drove the truck down to the church, and retrieved a med kit, blankets, and extra clothes that Saxton had stowed away in his truck's toolbox.

Geo whispered to Saxton, not expecting him to hear, "It's a good thing you are a park ranger, otherwise you'd be naked as a jaybird right now."

He had tugged Saxton up onto the pew and cleaned up all his wounds from the horrendous fight that had taken place not two hours earlier.

A large bandage covered the left side of his neck, a dull red haze showing at its center.

Geo had even found it necessary to jam Saxton's left arm back into joint. The beating he'd received from the black werewolf should have twisted it off like the wing of a fly.

He had managed to make a sling to put his arm in. He was no doctor and had no clue if it was actually broken, so he decided the sling would have to make do.

Geo felt as though he were being watched the whole time he had mended Saxton.

He knew the beast-man was near, but thankfully the edelweiss flower ground up and mixed with holy water had worked like a charm.

He placed its container on a leather strap and circled it around his neck, just in case he might need it later.

Geo looked up and down Saxton's covered torso and prayed he would not need the wolf mace anytime soon.

Another attack would be the death of his red headed friend, and probably his own, as well.

Assuring himself Saxton was asleep, he walked about the church, picking up anything that belonged to his fallen friend.

Behind the church's podium, there were long shreds of his clothes scattered throughout what was left of the choir loft.

166

He gathered up each strip of clothing as he came to it.

Under one of the choir pews, Geo could see a small flicker of light strobe in the darkness.

He bent down, his old knees crunching with the movement.

He slid his hand into the blackness and retrieved a cell phone.

Flipping open its cover, he read three missed calls labeled simply, *L. Daciana.*

"What a time for her to be calling," Geo whispered harshly.

He stepped forward in front of the podium, debating on what to do.

He knew calling her could be a mistake, but at the same time, she probably needed to know what had happened to Saxton.

Geo surveyed his surroundings, making sure he could see every possible opening for someone or something to get inside the rustic sanctuary.

He dialed the missed call and held his breath.

A woman picked up, without so much as a ring.

"Saxton, oh my God, are you okay?" Licah screamed through the small device.

"Um, Ms. Daciana? This isn't Saxton. I'm one of his friends, Geo. I'm up in Maine with him."

Licah sounded as though she were in hysterics, "Is he okay? Where is he?"

Geo tried to sound unalarmed, "He's with me, and he is resting."

Licah started to protest, but thought better of it, "I have been worried senseless! I know something is wrong with Saxton. My grandmother has been in the same state of mind I have been in. She says that Saxton and my grandfather are going to try and kill each other. She claims it's because Saxton is breaking into his territory by being there."

"You're grandfather? He was the other wolf?" Geo did not realize what he had said until it was too late.

"You mean you have seen him, my grandfather?" Licah pleaded.

Geo's mind raced for a way to tell Licah the truth without causing her more worry. However, after at least twenty seconds of silence he finally decided not to sugarcoat his tale.

"Ms. Daciana, we have seen your grandfather and you are correct, the two men were at each other's throats. Saxton is hurt, but I've got him patched up."

Licah began to weep with the hopelessness of the situation, the tears running down onto the phone, almost causing her to drop it. Her body was shaking so badly, she could barely speak, "Is…is he safe?"

Geo chose his words more carefully, "He is for the moment, but if the other wolf…I mean, your grandfather, comes back again, he won't be. I have a way to keep him at bay, but I have no clue how long it will last."

Licah tried to clear her mind enough to speak. The thought of Saxton hurt was too much for her to bear, "I have a way to stop him from turning into a werewolf when he's around me. The only problem is he has to be a wolf when I use it."

Geo's eyes widened, "You have the cure?"

Licah gave a resounding, "Yes!"

"Licah, I need you here in Bangor! If you have a way to prevent him from changing, I need you to be here and take care of him. That way I can do more snooping around, knowing he is safe."

Licah looked at her watch and started gathering her things together on the bed, "I can take a flight from Memphis and be there in about ten hours. Just keep Saxton safe and watch out for my grandfather."

Geo looked down at Saxton, "Thank you, Ms. Daciana. We will see you soon."

Geo clicked the phone shut and walked back to Saxton's side.

He could see that he was sleeping soundly by the movements of his chest, "Ten hours. I hope we are safe for that long."

Saxton twisted in his sleep at Geo's words.

Licah hurried down the airport terminal after exiting her flight. The place was strangely dim and cold. All the people around her seemed to move in slow motion as she ran past them to get to the rental car area.

She looked terrified. She bumped into a man in a business suit and knocked his briefcase from his hand. She twisted her head around and looked at him as if to say, "I'm sorry," but kept moving.

Licah could see the rental car area just ahead of her.

Having called ahead to make reservations, she ran to the terminal to retrieve the keys to her rental.

She quickly reversed course and headed for the double glass doors, to the parking lot.

Her senses appeared numbed, detached, as she ran through the automatic doors.

People were clustered together everywhere outside, making it hard to see which vehicle was hers.

There was a large group of men standing near the curb, leading back to the airport terminal.

She strained to see past them, trying to read the numbered signs next to the group of men.

She dashed in the direction of the men, but froze in her tracks.

The group turned and faced her, their movements muted and slowed.

The men parted in unison and revealed something that turned her blood to ice water.

There before her, standing on all fours, but still five feet high, was a gigantic black wolf.

Licah spun to sprint away, but it was no use. It was like her feet were buried in thick molasses.

She fell to the ground and quickly rolled to her back. She regained her senses just in time to see the black monster reach her feet.

It loomed above her, sharp teeth sparkling. A warm liquid dripped from it's fangs and onto her face.

She tried to scream when the beast bit down onto the meaty part of her throat, the sight of her own blood flooding her eyes like rain.

Saxton bolted awake, pulse racing double time. He rotated his head to see Geo standing over him.

By the look and size of his eyes, Geo knew the answer, "You were having a dream, son. Are you okay?"

He tried to speak, but his mouth was too dry. Saxton replied by giving a slight nod, the pain in his neck increasing.

"Go back to sleep. Help will hopefully be here soon."

Saxton closed his eyes again and thought to himself, "A dream? I pray that it was only a dream."

Chapter Eight

Licah gazed out the airplane window to see the Appalachian Mountains. Normally the view would stir her spirits, but her spirits were currently completely and utterly confused and terrified.

Confused because she had no idea why she was flying off to Maine to try to rescue a perfect stranger, especially knowing a ravenous werewolf was hanging around.

She only knew Saxton was her soul mate because her mother and grandmother had insisted that was what the mark meant.

She'd only had a few phone conversations with him and had only seen him face to face twice, well, three times if you considered the time when he was a wolf.

Why did life have to be so complicated?

She closed her eyes and tried to analyze how she felt about Saxton, but all she could come up with was...home.

She felt so drawn to him, always had.

Could she fall in love with a man she didn't even know?

Apparently she could.

She was terrified about what might happen when she landed in Maine. She knew they were around Bangor, but unless Geo could give her directions, she had no idea where she might end up.

She closed her eyes and tried not to think about it, but a face rose in her vision almost immediately.

Saxton.

His hair was only a few inches long and was simply styled to fall over his forehead. The color was a rich auburn that shined in the sun.

His gray eyes were rimmed in black, with just a speck of green near the pupil.

He had a smattering of freckles across his nose that she knew he felt made him look too young, but she found it very attractive.

His hands felt like satin, his fingers slightly roughened from working outside.

She could feel his touch and her heart yearned for it.

Her eyes popped open as she realized what she was doing.

She had never seen Saxton's hair in the sun. She had never been close enough to him to gaze into his eyes to note their color. And she'd most certainly never had his hands on her skin, especially not enough to yearn for it.

Maybe her mother and grandmother were right.

Maybe they were soul mates.

How else would she possibly know those things?

Licah held her breath as she stood at the rental counter at Bangor International Airport.

The young man behind the counter had been talking on his cell phone for over three minutes, laughing and cheering on his buddy who had apparently won tickets to some big football game for them both.

She cleared her throat loudly and watched as the young man glared at her and held up a finger for her to wait a minute.

Before she knew what she was doing, a growl crawled up her throat, and the young man looked at her in confusion.

She slammed her palm against the counter, hearing it crack under her hand.

"You listen to me, you Nici! My name is Licah Daciana, and I have a reservation. It is already paid for, just give me the damned keys!" she yelled, calling him the Romanian word for "punk".

The boy couldn't stop looking at her eyes as he reached with shaking hands to the computer.

She glanced up into the mirror behind the counter and took a step back when she realized her eyes were glowing.

Her eyes, normally emerald green, had taken on a yellowish hue and were shining like two penlights.

She closed her eyes and looked down.

She held out her hand.

"I'm sorry, just give me the keys."

She felt metal fall into her palm, and she looked back into the mirror and breathed deeply when she saw that her eyes were back to normal.

Maybe Saxton hadn't been the only one affected after all.

She'd have to ask her mother if it had ever happened to her.

She was pleasantly surprised when she found that the set of keys she received were to a cherry red Mazda RX-8.

She pulled out of the airport parking lot doing sixty, spinning tires and blacking up the pavement.

After she was through traffic and onto the interstate headed toward Metropolitan Bangor, she fumbled for her phone and called Geo.

The beautiful lights of Bangor at nighttime did little to appease her as she waited for an answer.

Geo lay planked out on one of the old church pews. His back felt as though someone had backed over him with a stream roller.

He had slept in worse conditions, but just couldn't remember where or when at that moment.

Flipping to this left side, Geo looked in the direction of Saxton, who was in the pew just in front of his.

He could hear him take in and release each breath. He sounded remarkably better compared to just a few hours before.

Geo pondered if he should have taken Saxton home after finding out about Licah having a cure for the curse.

However, he had a strange gut feeling that they should stay in Bangor, and his gut was rarely wrong.

He was still holding onto Saxton's cell phone when it sounded its musical ring tone, *Bad Moon Rising* by Credence Clearwater Revival.

"How fitting," Geo chuckled to himself. He answered the call to receive Licah, who sounded to be on the border of panic, "Licah, are you in Bangor?"

Saxton shot up from his pew at the mention of her name.

"I am, but I need directions to where you two are, and I need to talk to Saxton, now!"

Her abruptness took Geo by surprise. Without a word, he handed the phone to Saxton.

Saxton's voice was soft and almost lyrical, "Licah, are you okay? I have been having terrible nightmares."

"I'm fine, really I am," her voice shaking as the words left her mouth. "Geo told me you were attacked. Please tell me that you are okay. I have been worried senseless."

Saxton reached up to feel the bandage on his neck and realized he was doing it with his left hand.

Just a few hours before, he couldn't even move that arm. He lightly tapped the bandage and realized that his pain was completely gone.

With surprise in his voice, he replied, "I am feeling much better, especially after hearing from you."

The other end of the phone went silent for a moment while Licah tried to sort out her feelings.

Tears began rolling down her cheeks as she spoke with emotion, "I was afraid you had been killed, *dragul meu*," saying 'my love' in her family's native tongue.

Saxton was shocked at Licah's tears. How could this woman, that didn't even know him, be so distraught over him being hurt? But he also understood, his feelings for her burned as hot as a candle's blue flame.

"Really, I am okay. Please don't cry. Those beautiful green eyes will get all puffy, and I'll not be able to see them very well if they are swollen shut," he chuckled, trying his best to lift her spirits.

She chuckled.

Saxton's tone stayed soft, but was filled with seriousness, "Sweetie, I don't know what's going to happen in all this, but please know right now, if we manage to get out of this alive, I want to be with you," Saxton's own words even shocked himself.

He almost regretted his admission until Licah spoke back, "We are going to get out of this situation just fine. I have the amulet. And I want to be with you too."

She held the amulet in her hand, the chain wrapped around her wrist, as she drove.

"I just needed you to know, just in case something were to happen to me," Saxton felt his own heart melt.

Licah's heart palpitated at the thought.

"Don't say things like that! You will be fine. Now, tell me how to get to you."

Saxton explained he didn't exactly know and handed the phone back to Geo.

While they spoke, he had time to think about what he had said to Licah.

"Do I really care that much about a woman I don't even know? I only recall seeing her twice in my life and that was over eighteen years ago. How can this be real?" he quietly asked himself in complete sincerity.

Saxton snapped back into reality as Geo snapped the cell phone shut, "She should be here any minute."

Licah watched as the city lights slowly dimmed to nothing.

She followed Geo's directions to the letter. They took her to an old church.

She whipped the vehicle into the parking lot, and gasped in fear when her headlights hit the church steps. There, at the foot of them, stood the beast.

A black nightmare come to life.

He was bigger than a wolf, his limbs shaped differently, and he was nearly the size of a man.

His stance on the steps betrayed that he was ready to spring at any moment.

Her heart began to race, and the mark on her chest began to burn worse than it ever had.

She looked to the small church and knew that Saxton was in there. She didn't know how, but she knew.

She looked again at the beast and noticed it still hadn't moved.

Its feral blue gaze seemed to burn right into her soul, and she suddenly couldn't breathe.

So this was her grandfather.

A man who should love her and keep her safe, but his slathering fangs told her differently.

She cut the ignition and took a deep breath.

She picked up her cell phone and dialed Saxton's number.

"Are you okay?" he answered on the first ring.

"Yes, I'm outside the church, but my grandfather is guarding the door."

"I knew you were close, my heart is racing and my chest is burning. If you come any closer, I'm going to change, and Geo will be in danger," he replied with a breathy voice.

She started the car and backed into a parking lot space as far away from the church as she could.

"Is that better? I'm in the parking lot next to the church," she asked, hoping the small distance would ease him.

She heard him take a deep breath and he said, "Yes, it's not burning as bad now."

"Saxton, I don't know what to do."

Saxton turned to Geo and looked deeply into his old friend's eyes.

"Hang on, baby. I'm coming to get you."

Geo's eyes widened as he watched Saxton hang up the phone.

"What's your plan?" he asked, getting up from the pew he'd been reclining on.

Saxton looked around at the stained glass windows and shook his head.

"I'm going to go out front and distract her grandfather, while you go around back and get her. She's in the lot next to the church."

Geo's pale face blanched even further, and he shook his head.

"That wolf will kill you, and you know it."

Saxton laughed.

"The last time, she wasn't here for me to fight for."

Licah grabbed her purse and backpack. She normally packed to the gills for trips, but she had been in such a hurry to get to Saxton, she'd just thrown some clothes and necessities in the school-like backpack and had run.

She wanted to be ready for whatever Saxton had planned.

She watched the wolf closely. She knew he would know Saxton was coming before she would.

"Come on, baby," she said more to herself than anything.

She noticed a light near the back of the church and saw an older man walk out and crouch near some bushes, an odd looking bottle in his hand.

She saw him lift a phone to his ear, and her cell phone rang.

"Saxton is going to transform inside the church, I need you to pull the car up as close as you can, but as far away from that wolf as possible."

Licah's eyebrows crinkled.

She looked over the parking lot and saw that there was enough space to get the car right beside Geo.

She started the car again and moved slowly toward him, watching the wolf all the while.

The creature watched her, his shaggy black head turning, but his body staying deathly still.

"Good girl, now, stay there. Saxton is going to change..."

Before Geo could get the words out, the wolf's head whipped around just as another werewolf, this one ginger in color, burst out the front door and pounced on the black wolf.

Licah watched in horror as they became a blur of claws and teeth, falling down the steps and into the small yard.

"Now, girl, now, run to the back door!" Geo yelled.

Licah didn't think, she just reacted.

She cut the ignition, grabbed her bags and fled from the car to where Geo was standing.

The old man grabbed her by the arm and rushed her into the mudroom of the church.

"What now? How can we help him?" she exclaimed, running into the sanctuary of the church toward the front door.

"Stop, stay here. There was no sense in him risking his life for you to go out there and risk your own."

She looked at him incredulously.

"I have to risk my life, or I can't be with him while he's human. That's the way this amulet works. I have to put it around his neck while he's a wolf!" she screamed.

Geo walked up to her and put his hands on her trembling shoulders.

"Licah, stay here. Let me go out there. I may be able to make them snap out of it."

Having no idea what the man had planned, she decided she was too upset to argue.

She sat down on a pew, trying to ignore the snarls from the front door.

She watched as Geo walked toward the church's entrance. The bottle he had been holding earlier was held firmly in his hand.

Afraid to witness what was about to happen just outside, she quickly turned away. She lowered her head, placed her hands near her face, and began a prayer.

Geo walked like a man headed into oblivion.

The sounds from just in front of him did not frighten him. He had dealt with supernatural occurrences many times in his life. No matter how peculiar each occurrence was, he lusted for the high that came along with it.

He could feel his heart begin to push his blood hurriedly through his body. His vision and hearing were at top performance. Even his sense of smell had amplified to the point that he could smell the two beasts while they bounded to and fro, trying to avoid each other's claws and teeth.

Geo neared the broken front doors, and readjusted the makeshift mace container in his hand.

He stood at the top of the old stone steps and patiently watched the beasts trying to wear one another down.

Geo stood like a statue and waited for just the right moment to strike at the black beast not ten feet away.

The black wolf seemed to be toying with the younger wolf, allowing him to get just close enough for an attack. Then it would leap into the air and land on its four paws with an earth-shaking thud a couple of feet away.

It happened all at once.

The red wolf leapt for the other's throat only to be catapulted in the air by a giant black paw.

Saxton landed in a heap just at the bottom of the steps. The black giant pounced with the accuracy of a lion and wrapped its razor sharp teeth around his neck.

Geo flew with cheetah-like speed to the bottom of the stone steps, mace bottle in hand.

Just as the black beast's front canines opened the other wolf's throat, Geo loaded the monster's muzzle with the opaque liquid.

It howled in pain, its mouth letting go of the other wolf's flesh, but not before blood splattered up Geo's arm.

Geo drew back quickly, cursing at the colossal wolf.

He awaited a counterattack, but one did not come.

Instead, the black beast fled, howling and snarling as it crossed the weathered road, disappearing into the dark tree line.

Licah could hear the sounds of agony from behind her. She had no clue if it was her grandfather or Saxton that was in pain.

Her emotions were to their peak. Her sadness and fear were suddenly replaced with determination and anger.

She couldn't just sit there and let Saxton die.

She knew deep within her very soul that she loved him, even though he was more or less a stranger to her.

Standing, she could feel the anger building inside herself.

Reaching into her belongings, she retrieved the amulet and held it firmly in her grasp. Just across from her hung a large, dirt-spattered picture of Mary holding the infant Jesus in her arms.

A strange yellowish green glow reflected from the picture's glass. It took Licah only a second to realize it was her own glowing eyes that were the source of the light.

Licah could feel the now ever-present burning of her scar begin to slowly diminish.

At first she thought it meant that Saxton had moved farther away.

This new feeling, however, was different... hollowing.

"My God, he's dying!"

Spinning around, Licah faced the church's front door. She could feel the anger building inside of her at the thought of any harm coming to her *dragul meu.*

She bolted to the door with a courage she had never experienced in her entire existence.

The courage equaled the love that burned within her, a burn that was slowly fading into darkness.

She could hear Geo yelling as the church's steps came into her view.

She paused at the top of the steep, stone steps and peered downward.

At their foot stood Geo, his limbs firmly rooted to the ground under him.

His right arm was extended outward, as far as he could reach, elbow locked into place.

She could make out a large bloodstain on his arms and body that made her tremble in fear.

He spun around on his aging legs at the sight of Licah's approach.

At Geo's feet lay a large red colored wolf, blood covering most of its upper torso.

It was as still as death.

Licah ran to the wolf's side.

She knew it was Saxton. She knelt down next to him and placed her hand on his chest.

She could barely feel his breathing, so she moved her hand to his fur covered wrist, looking for a pulse.

After several seconds, Licah was able to find a weak heartbeat.

She bent down further to wrap her arms around her beast, knowing full well the teeth inches from her neck could kill her in a heartbeat.

Geo broke the silence, his breath labored from exhaustion and excitement, "We need to get him to a hospital."

Licah turned and glared at him, "And how do you suppose I get him to a hospital? If I am with you, he will look like this!"

Geo motioned to the object in her hand, "Put it on him, now. Be quick about it!" Geo's stance loosened, and he lost his balance.

Licah started to reach out to stop his fall, but he righted himself.

"Put the damned amulet on him, before it's too late!" Geo yelled, his voice sounding broken.

Leaning over him, she put the amulet around Saxton's hairy neck.

There, before her very eyes, he began to change back into his normal self. The hair all over his body seemed to almost burn away.

She leaned even closer once the transformation was complete and silently willed her soul mate to heal.

She had no idea if it would work, so she spoke point blank to Geo, but her caress never left Saxton's lifeless body, "We mustn't let him die! For God's sake, help me get him in my car!"

Geo walked around to one side of Saxton and bent down to help Licah lift him up, "If he doesn't get help soon, he's gonna bleed to death," his voice vibrating in fear.

As they lifted Saxton up, she chimed in, "Not on my watch, he won't!"

Chapter Nine

Licah held Saxton in her arms, while Geo drove the little Mazda.

He was hell-bent on getting his friend to a hospital.

Saxton's chest looked like hamburger and his neck, like a gnawed beaver log.

Licah's eyes were still glowing as she felt his too-slow heartbeat.

"Saxton, baby, just hold on. We're going to get you help."

He appeared to stir at her voice and took a deep labored breath.

The wheeze she had been hearing silenced, and suddenly he began coughing.

Blood poured from his lips and onto Licah's jacket.

Licah didn't know what to do, so she quickly removed the blazer and used it to mop the blood from his face.

"Licah," he whispered.

She realized the wheeze had vanished when he spoke her name.

Her brow loosened and she looked up, meeting Geo's gaze in the rearview mirror.

"He's healing, Geo! I'm sure his lungs were punctured, but his wheezing stopped, and he just expelled the blood that had collected in them. I don't understand, but he's miraculously healing."

She brushed the red strands of Saxton's hair across his forehead and gently pressed her hand to his cheek.

He felt feverish, and his freckled cheeks were flushed.

"Licah," he whispered again, turning his head from side to side.

She tried to stop him, afraid he would tear the wound in his neck even more.

She passed her fingertips over the gash, but felt none. Only Saxton's soft, smooth skin remained.

She frowned.

"Geo, I don't think we're going to need a hospital. He's healing so fast."

Geo slowed from bat out of hell to moderately illegal speed and looked at her in the mirror.

"What do you want to do?"

Licah shook her head and lightly dabbed Saxton's naked chest, watching his skin knit together.

"We need to go somewhere private, not a hotel."

Geo sat for a moment and seemed to perk up.

"If we can find a phone book, we can call my friend Will. He's actually the one we came to see."

Licah looked at Geo in disbelief and held up her cell phone.

"I don't need a phone book. I can get the internet on my phone."

As Geo ranted about young people and modern technology, Licah surfed the web on her cell phone to a phone number listing website.

"What's his last name?" she asked absentmindedly keying in Will as the first name.

"Serban," Geo replied, turning into a rest area.

Licah looked up in surprise.

"Willard Serban?" she exclaimed.

Geo looked oddly at her and nodded.

Licah's breath caught in her throat.

"Willard Serban is my grandfather."

Licah nonchalantly approached the counter at the rattiest motel she'd ever been in.

An older woman with mustard stains on her wife-beater shirt blew out a puff of smoke at her approach.

Licah considered the possibility that the woman had never heard of a bra, but thought it unlikely.

"I need a room with two beds please," she asked, pushing a credit card across the counter.

The woman smiled, showing off a few yellowed teeth, "Cash only."

Licah smiled back tightly and put her credit card back in her pocket.

"How much?" Licah asked, fishing in her back pocket, hoping what little cash she had would be enough.

"Forty," the lady replied, thumping a fly from the counter.

Licah suddenly wasn't so worried about getting blood on the sheets.

She pulled out two twenties and passed them across the counter.

The lady snatched the money in a wad and stuffed it in her cleavage.

She took a key from a pegboard on the wall, "Number seven, round back."

Licah didn't bother to reply, but shivered in her thin t-shirt as she walked outside, her jacket was still with Saxton in the backseat.

Geo had parked the Mazda at the very end of the gravel parking lot, so that no one would see Saxton in the back.

She gestured toward the back of the building. Geo followed her in the car and stopped just short of the room.

She glanced back and forth while opening the door, then was thankful the smell of the room wasn't overwhelming.

After making sure there wasn't anyone around, she helped Geo take Saxton into the motel room.

He was actually able to half-support himself as they walked across the carpet to one of the double beds.

Licah left Geo to support Saxton. She rushed to the bathroom to wet a towel with warm water.

Geo eased Saxton to a sitting position, and waited for Licah to return, "I need to go talk to Will."

Licah had known it was coming, so she just nodded. She had more important things on her mind at that moment.

She rattled off the address she had found on her phone after the initial shock had worn off, and tossed him the keys from the nightstand.

"Take the keys, we're not going anywhere, but bring my purse and my bags in."

Geo left the room to comply. She helped Saxton lie down on the comforter.

His body was still covered in blood, but most of the wounds were healed. But she knew that his insides were still knitting together by the painful faces he made as he reclined back.

"Just lie still, I'm going to try to clean you up a bit."

She started to wipe the blood clean from his chest, and was suddenly very aware that he was naked on a bed.

His eyes watched her as she cleaned the blood from his thick chest hair, and she began to go lower.

When she got close to his navel, his hand stopped her.

She looked up at him and met his gaze.

They stared at each other for a long moment before Saxton asked, "Will you help me into the shower?"

Geo let the motel room door close behind him, and trotted off to acquire Licah's belongings.

A thousand different things ran through his mind as he opened the car and retrieved the items requested.

He smiled when his mind stopped to ponder what would transpire while he went to find Willard.

It was probably best he made himself scarce for a while anyway. No use in being a third wheel.

Bags in hand, Geo walked back to the room and opened the door just enough to place Licah's things through the crack.

As the door slowly closed under its own weight he spoke, "Saxton, if I run into any trouble, I will call. I still have your cell phone."

Without waiting for a reply, Geo returned to the Mazda and sped away, top speed.

He looked down at his wristwatch fearing what he'd see. Days had passed since he'd gotten his usual amount of sleep. "Almost three in the morning," he groaned.

But Geo was not sleepy by any means. He was too hyped up with the past few hours' events to even feel the slightest tug of fatigue.

His biggest concern was the amount of energy he would have available to him, just in case he were to run into any trouble.

Geo followed the curvy back roads, and his thoughts turned to Willard and the black wolf.

Thinking loudly, he spoke, "So, Will has been a part of this the entire time? Why the hell didn't he tell me?"

But it all made sense. He and Will had become friends after doing research together on various supernatural subjects, and when Will moved away years ago, Geo knew it was an abrupt change for his friend to make.

Will kept to himself, showing no interest in having many people around, save Geo. He was a lonely man who had very few visitors.

The only person Will ever spoke of from his private life was Lila, the love of his life.

Geo always assumed she was his deceased wife or long lost girlfriend because he talked about her like she was with him, but not with him.

The way he spoke of her insinuated that their days together had been cut short or soon would be.

Pulling the Mazda in front of the church, Geo peered at the front steps. Puddled at the foot was a large pool of blood—Saxton's blood.

It was indeed miraculous that the boy survived his battle with Will after losing that much blood.

Geo shook his head in disbelief and thankfulness.

Now, to find Will.

It dawned on Geo because he had left the motel in such haste that he forgot to bring the address that Licah had given him. However, he did remember seeing a few houses that looked to still have residents.

Backing the car out, he headed west, up the nearly abandoned road. He could make out a couple of houses with lights on inside them.

He debated on going to each door and asking for Will, but thought better of it.

Nearing the end of the road, one house caught his eye. Not because it looked any differently designed than the others, but mainly because the front light was on and the door was standing open.

Maine in September at three o'clock in the morning was not somewhere you would expect to find this unless, of course, the residents wanted to freeze to death.

Geo pulled the car up the short driveway.

The white paint of the small, wooden house magnified by the headlights.

There on the first porch was a man, laying half inside the front door.

Exiting the car, Geo surveyed his surroundings.

He wondered if the wolf had jumped an unsuspecting person on his way across town.

He cautiously approached the front porch.

The man's body was face down and he was completely naked. The top half of his body lay over the door's threshold.

He rolled him over and discovered his old friend Willard.

Geo felt Will's pulse, and it was calm and steady.

He seemed to have no physical damage from the fight earlier.

He grabbed him under his arms and slowly pulled him into the house. The metal-framed, glass door closed behind him with a slam.

After helping him into a chair, Geo grabbed a quilt that sat on a nearby couch and tossed it over Will.

He had no idea how long it would take him to recover from his transformation, so he sat on the couch, picked up the remote to the television and switched it on.

He placed his feet on the coffee table, "Maybe there is something good on the History Channel."

Within minutes, an exhausted Geo was sound asleep.

The television remote hit the floor with a loud thud, and he jerked awake.

He twisted his position in the chair to face Will. He appeared to still be asleep. The blanket that Geo had thrown over him was wrapped tightly around him.

"He must have stirred at least a little to make himself more comfortable," Geo thought.

Will's dark-colored quilt nearly blended with his hair. The dark shades made his fair skin look a ghostly white.

Geo stood and approached Will with caution.

He had no idea what state of mind he would find his old friend in.

As he approached, his foot set off a loud pop in the floor's old hardwood.

He stopped and cursed at the sound.

Will jerked awake, his eyes wide and his breathing heavy.

After the initial shock, he narrowed his eyes to get a bead on his intruder.

His face lightened and his mouth popped open in surprise, "Geo! What the hell? When did you get here? How did you find me?"

Geo walked up to his old friend and stood directly in front of him, "It's been a long time, Will," his eyes smiling on his old research buddy.

Will sprang to his feet, and gave Geo a gigantic bear hug. His quilt fell to his feet and Geo quickly broke the embrace, "I think you need to get dressed, so we can talk."

Will quickly grabbed up the timeworn quilt and turned away from his old friend, "So, you know now?"

Geo looked at him with a stern, yet concerned look, "Why didn't you ever tell me? After all the stuff we have done and seen in the past, I would have been the first to understand and maybe even help."

Will rotated away from his old friend, ashamed to meet Geo's gaze, "My story...my hurt...it ran too deep for me to explain. It still hurts to this day."

Geo could make out the sign of a tear coming from the corner of his eye. He placed his hand on his left shoulder, trying to catch his gaze, "Go get cleaned up, and we will talk."

Will shuffled into the bathroom and closed the door.

Geo sat back down on the couch and was pondering all the incredible, recent events when he heard the shower turn on.

Geo wondered exactly what his oldest friend would have to tell him that was so hurtful.

His mind also went to how Saxton and Licah were dealing with his problem. A smile flashed across his lips.

Saxton wasn't feeling his best, but Licah's touch set him on fire.

He knew she noticed the effect her cleaning efforts had on him; it was hard not to notice.

Licah's small pink tongue shot out and she licked her lips.

Saxton ached to feel that tongue pass his lips and into his mouth.

She nodded and handed him the towel, woodenly getting to her feet and marching to the bathroom.

Saxton looked down at his erection and shook his head.

He knew it wasn't the time or the place, but his body didn't seem to be listening.

He heard the sound of the shower hitting the porcelain tub and looked at Licah standing in the bathroom doorway.

She stood there looking so vulnerable and unsure of herself.

He finished wiping off the blood, trying to calm his body, and shakily stood up.

He wrapped the bloody towel around his waist and walked over to her.

She wouldn't look into his eyes, and his heart ached to see their emerald depths again.

"Licah, I need you to know something."

She slowly met his gaze, and he felt his heartbeat triple.

The amulet around his neck began to burn, and he thanked whatever higher power there was that someone had made the thing.

"I've waited so long to do this; I can't seem to restrain myself."

With that he leaned over and captured her lips with his own.

God, she tasted like heaven.

Her lips were feather-soft, and he growled at the taste of her.

Licah had never felt such desire in her entire life.

Saxton's hands fanned through her hair and he clasped the back of her neck, plunging his tongue past her lips.

Her knees went weak when he pushed her back against the wall.

She reached up, ran her fingers through his chest hair, and deepened their kiss.

He pulled back from her and closed his eyes, resting his forehead against her own.

"I'm sorry," he whispered, his breath ragged.

She shook her head.

"No, I'm sorry. You're hurt, and I shouldn't be making advances."

He looked to her in surprise.

"I'm not that hurt."

She laughed and wrapped her arms around his waist, lying her head on his chest, not caring that he was still partially covered in blood.

"The water's getting cold," she whispered into his chest.

"Are you going to join me?" he asked.

She looked up into his eyes again and was surprised when his gaze held not only lust, but the love she had searched for her entire life.

Wearing a tattered, gray robe and a towel draped over his head, Will exited his bedroom.

He felt rejuvenated after his shower.

Sitting down in his chair, he took the towel and began drying the last bit of water out of his hair.

Will looked at Geo, who was staring at him inquisitively.

It had been decades since he had transformed into his beastly self.

He had very few memories of the night before, other than the burning sensation that came to his old scar.

He really had nothing to tell his old friend other than the events from ages ago.

He smirked at Geo and laughed as he inhaled a deep breath, "You have always smelled strange for a human, Geo."

Geo grinned at his friend's humor, but quickly returned to serious mode, "So, are you gonna tell me about this, or are we gonna to play twenty questions?"

Will adjusted in his seat, "I'm afraid there's not much to tell that you probably haven't figured out on your own."

Geo frowned at him, "I found some of your books on the subject that you gave me years ago. This family curse you are a part of, *Blestemul Vârcolac de Dragoste*, the Werewolf Curse of Love."

"Then what do you need me to tell you? It should have been all there, laid out in black and white."

He could tell that Will had no intention of making this easy, "Would it loosen up your lips a little if I told you that your granddaughter is here in Bangor?"

Will rose to his feet, "Licah is here? Oh my God, is that why I transformed last night? I don't remember much about what happened. Did I hurt her?"

Geo motioned him back to his seat, "No, you didn't. But I don't think it was Licah. You see, her soul mate is here too."

Will's face went pale, and his palms began to sweat.

His eyes moved about the room, trying to find the words to ask Geo, "Did...did I hurt him?" He threw his face into his palms.

"He's okay. He's with Licah now and..."

"But how? He'll slash her to pieces!"

Geo shook his head, "No, we have the amulet. She managed to get it on him after the two of you fought."

"Maybe you should tell me all that has happened, and I will fill you in on what I know of the curse."

Geo agreed and began the tale, starting with the autumn of ninety-three.

He explained all that had been told to him by Saxton, trying hard not to leave anything out.

Will grew reflective, reliving his own experience of ages ago, as he listened to Geo's tale.

Once Geo had finished giving him the details up to present day, Will seemed to deflate.

The fire of worry in his dark eyes had been replaced with a river of despair, "If you have the amulet, then there isn't much else I know to tell you. That is the only way to stop her soul mate from turning into a wolf."

Geo studied his old friend's eyes carefully, "Are you so sure? Maybe if we got in touch with Licah's grandmother she could..."

Will erupted in an emotional rage, "No! I will not call Lila!"

He fell on his knees and began sobbing into his towel, "It...it hurts too much to speak to her."

Geo came to his friend's side, helping him back to his seat.

He remained by the arm of his chair and placed his weathered hand on Will's shoulder, hoping to comfort him.

Will softly continued, "I miss her more than you could ever understand or imagine, Geo. There is not a moment of time that goes by that I don't think about her."

The wistfulness on his face nearly broke Geo's heart.

"She came to me when I was in the service, where I nearly died. When I first turned into the wolf, she knew what to do. She gave me the amulet, and it never happened again until the night we parted ways. It was the night that our daughter, Anca, was conceived."

Geo looked at his friend, confused, "Why that night in particular?"

Will drew in a hard, deep breath between his tears, "Because, that was the night I mistakenly removed the amulet when I was in her presence and I..."

Geo finished it for him, "...and you turned back into the wolf."

Geo could barely understand his words as he shouted, "I almost killed her! The one thing in this world, the only true thing I would have given my life for. I'd give anything for just a single day to be with her again. Damned this curse...it drove her away from me, and damn you for making me remember it!"

He shoved Geo's hand off his shoulder and reached beside his chair to reveal a pint-sized bottle of Tennessee whiskey. He removed the cap and took a deep drink.

Geo snatched the bottle from his grasp.

Willard didn't try to fight him. He just pressed his face back into his hands, his bath towel soaked in tears.

"I need the phone number for Lila. She may have a clue on what we can do."

He sat back up, his tear-stained cheeks glowing like hot embers, "We only talk on the anniversary of the day we met. She won't take my calls otherwise."

Geo was getting impatient, "Just give me the number, and I will call her!"

He spoke the number like he had dialed it a million times.

Pulling out Saxton's cell phone, he dialed the number. Granted it was in the wee hours of the morning, but it couldn't wait.

The phone rang once, again, and again. The sound of a sleepy woman answered on the other end. Her voice was coarse, as though she might have been crying.

"May I speak to Lila, please?"

"Who is calling at this hour?" Lila was not pleased, her Romanian accent making the words seem harsher than they normally would have.

Geo could see that Will was reacting to her voice and retreated to the kitchen, "My name is George Riner. I am an acquaintance of Licah. I really could use your help..."

"Oh, my dear Licah, is she okay?"

Geo could hear her moving around, sounding like she had risen from her bed.

"She is fine. I am trying to help her. I know about the curse, and I know about Willard."

The phone went silent.

A rapid string of Romanian came through the phone into Geo's ear as a deafening ring.

"Lila, I really need your help in this. I am trying to find a cure for her."

"There is no cure, only the amulet."

"I think there may be a way to reverse the curse, but I need you to send me everything that you know about it. If I am correct, I may be able to end this so no one else has to suffer."

Lila went silent again as she mulled over the risk in trusting this complete stranger, "You can really help her?"

Geo smiled, "I am doing everything in my power to try."

Lila took a deep breath, building up the strength to discuss the subject, "I have papers and old documents that may help you. I have looked into this myself, but have never found a way to break the wolf's curse."

"Could you overnight them to me? I will pay whatever it costs to get them to me as fast as you can."

"I am not worried about the costs, just help my granddaughter. Help her not have to go through the pain that I have endured all these years. I don't want her to have to live with a broken heart like I have."

Geo grinned with pleasure, "Thank you Lila. I will do whatever it takes to end this curse once and for all. Can you have the documents sent to the airport in Bangor? I know they have a same day mailing service there."

"I will and please, be careful. Don't let the wolf destroy you like it almost destroyed me."

At that moment, Will barged into the room, "I must talk to Lila! Please, let me talk to her!"

He grabbed it out of Geo's hand so fast the cell phone went flying across the room, landing on the hard linoleum floor. Pieces of it showered the room, as it broke apart.

Will dropped to the floor, scraping the plastic shards into his hands, "No! My Lila, I must see you. I must touch you again." His weeping burned Geo's ears.

Knowing Will was exhausted, he led him to his bedroom and sat him on his bed, "Willard, I've got to go, but please understand, I am going to help you, somehow. It was good to see you after all these years. I will be back soon. Just don't give up!"

Geo closed the bedroom door and headed to the car, "I need to check on Saxton and Licah to make sure he hasn't tried to take her apart."

Saxton leaned against the counter as he watched Licah watch him.

She reached for the hem of her t-shirt and lifted it to show the most gorgeous expanse of female flesh he'd ever laid his eyes on.

Her bra was a light pink lace that complimented her olive skin.

She unbuttoned her jeans and slowly slid them down her long slender legs, revealing the matching bikini panties beneath.

Saxton's mouth went dry as she gazed at him, while reaching to unhook her bra.

As if on cue, he advanced toward her. He placed his hands on her slender arms to stop her motions. He leaned into her, his lips lightly dragging across hers.

He carefully and delicately passed his hands down her back, looking into her emerald eyes.

They appeared as two black moons, highlighted with a ring of jade.

Saxton's fingers found their destination, the clasp of her bra.

Still studying her face, the pink-laced article fell to her feet.

He slightly grinned at her, which she returned, almost looking away. Taking his left hand, he caressed her cheek, not wanting to lose her gaze.

After several moments, Saxton looked away from Licah's face to admire her shapely curves.

Her breasts stood erect and trembled under his observation. He wanted to run his hands from her back and across her nipples, but not yet.

There was still so much more of her body to admire before getting to that point.

Leaning forward again, he began kissing the side of her neck.

She inhaled deeply when he reached just above her shoulder.

Licah pulled away from him.

Saxton, thinking he had erred in some way, pulled back to look at her.

Unbeknownst to him, she had run her thumbs into the top edging of her panties. She bent quickly to push the garment to her feet.

Saxton scanned her alluringly, slowly admiring her curves. His gaze never locked onto a certain area for very long.

He wanted to appreciate all of her.

He took her by her right hand, and whispered for her to follow.

Leading her toward the bathroom door, he let his towel fall to the floor. His body made it perfectly clear what it wanted.

Licah looked Saxton up and down, her cheeks glowing with excitement at seeing his naked body.

He led her into the bathroom and motioned for her to step to the shower.

She complied and he followed suit. He stood with the front of his body pressed up against the back of hers.

The water felt cold, even though it was obvious by the steam swirling about the room that it was not.

Saxton wrapped his long arms around her petite frame and the water rained down upon them.

The hint of blood came off his body and rolled down the shower's drain, the last remnant of his earlier battle.

He leaned toward her ear, his arms locked around her chest. He softly whispered, "I never thought I'd be able to touch you like this, ever."

Looking down at his chest, Saxton noted the amulet pressed between the two of them, "Thank God for whoever made you!"

Tears began to roll down his cheeks, covered by the showers spray.

Licah looked up at him, her face suddenly filled with concern.

He took a hand, wiped away the saltiness from his face, and smiled, "I'm okay, baby. It's just that I have dreamt of this moment for over eighteen years."

Licah pressed her body harder into his, causing him to tighten his grip around her tiny olive frame.

Saxton looked down the front of her body and saw the scar left by the curse above her left breast.

He began to trace his finger along its outline.

She quivered at his touch.

It was as though all the blood from her heart raced to that one spot.

Saxton could feel her trembling at his touch and inquired, "You okay?"

Licah nodded boldly, "It's so intense when you touch me there."

She delicately pulled away from his body, just enough to turn and face him. She molded her torso with his, her breasts against his wet body.

Looking at his mark, she whispered, "May I try?"

Saxton nodded in response.

Licah lightly ran the back of her hand across his paw shaped marking.

He inhaled a breath that seemed to pull all the steam from the air.

She smiled, "You like that?"

Saxton grinned and nodded, "If that is this intense, I can only imagine what other things will feel like."

Licah face flushed a light pink. Her eyes were wide, anticipating his next move.

She finally spoke, "Who needs to imagine?"

Geo was halfway to the hotel when he realized what he might be barging into.

He decided to listen at the door and if he heard anything other than snarls, he would get his own room in the motel, far away from Saxton and Licah.

But not too far.

Licah reached over and grabbed the small wrapped bar of soap the motel had graciously provided and unwrapped it, letting the paper fall to the shower floor.

She pointedly avoided Saxton's gaze as she lathered up her hands and began running them all over her body.

Saxton's breathing quickened, and she hid a smile by bending over to wash her long legs.

As she rose back up, she made sure he noticed that her eyes admired his form and that she was pleased that he was so ready for her.

She lathered up her hands again and began at his shoulders, soaping up his broad chest and down his lean stomach.

When she reached for his waist, she finally met his gaze only to see that his head was thrown back and his eyes were closed, his mouth slightly open.

She reached for him and took him into her hands, his indrawn breath nearly pulling him away.

She gently cleansed him and touched his shoulder.

When his gray eyes met hers, she leaned forward and captured his lips.

Saxton went into action, lifting her from the shower floor.

Licah wrapped her long legs around his waist, and Saxton moved them both under the spray to wash the last of the soap away.

They were both completely soaked, but their kiss never broke.

It only became more passionate, more desperate.

Saxton reached over and turned off the water, supporting Licah with one hand on her firm bottom.

As they departed the shower, Saxton nearly slipped, but righted himself quickly, never breaking their kiss.

With Licah still in his arms, he escorted her to the main room where they collapsed onto one of the beds.

He finally pulled away and looked into her emerald depths.

"Are you sure this is what you want?"

He watched as she reached up to the amulet around his neck, its leather cord soaked.

"I've never been so sure of anything in my life."

Geo pulled up to the hotel room and was pleased to see that the door was still intact.

He got out of the Mazda and decided not to listen in.

They both needed time together.

He walked around the motel exterior to the office.

Saxton reached behind him and uncurled Licah's legs from his waist.

He ran his hand along the silky length of her leg, scratching delicately with his nails.

She closed her eyes and sighed at his touch.

He nipped her neck with his teeth, and she turned her head to give him better access.

"You are the most beautiful woman I've ever seen," he whispered in her ear before running his tongue down the column of her throat.

He cupped her breast in his hand, toying with its peak.

She gasped at his touch, and her back arched lightly.

He took it into his mouth and suckled her until she writhed underneath him.

"Saxton, please," she begged.

A very masculine grin spread across his face as he kissed his way down her stomach and settled between her legs.

Just as she opened her eyes to see why he had stopped, he plunged his tongue into her sweet core, and she cried out his name.

He slipped a finger into her warm wet depths and began rubbing just inside.

After only a few more flicks of his tongue, her whole body tightened and shattered into a thousand pieces.

Before she could catch her breath, he was on top of her, kissing her gasps away.

She reached between them and guided him into her.

They both moaned as he buried himself inside her and began a rhythm as old as time itself.

She ran her nails down his back and tried desperately not to hurt him.

The fire running through her body was like nothing she had ever felt before.

Saxton knelt back on his knees, bringing her with him, still impaled on his lap.

Her weight was nothing to him, and he continued his rhythm while kissing her desperately.

She pushed him back on the bed and straddled his waist.

He grabbed her hands, and she used them as leverage as she rode him until she felt her body burst in release.

After two more thrusts, Saxton threw his head back and moaned, spilling himself deep inside her.

Licah collapsed on top of him and tried to find her breath, still feeling the tremors of release running through both their bodies.

"Oh, my God," he whispered, brushing her hair out of her face.

She could only nod with her head on his chest.

They lay there for several minutes just basking in their union.

Licah traced his mark with her finger, and she finally said, "Saxton, thank you. No matter what happens, just know that tonight means so much to me."

He touched her chin and turned her face toward him.

"Licah, marry me?"

Chapter Ten

Saxton watched Licah sleep as the sun ascended the horizon.

He couldn't believe she'd said yes. She hadn't even hesitated.

She lay on her stomach, her face turned toward him on the pillow.

They'd made love again, this time slowly, and she'd fallen asleep with her hand resting over his mark.

He couldn't explain the feelings coursing through him.

He knew now that they were soul mates. Nothing else could explain their bond.

He wondered about Geo, but decided he would worry about his old friend in a few hours.

He reached for Licah and nestled her head in the crook of his arm.

Right then there was nothing more important than holding her.

Of feeling her body against his and knowing that for that moment, all was right in their world.

225

He closed his eyes, vowing to do whatever it took to make her safe.

Willard lay motionless in his bed, the occasional tear rolling down the side of his face.

He pondered all the events that had brought Geo to his door.

He figured he would never see his old friend again after that night.

Another tear rolled down his face, this one landing in his ear.

He knew all his thoughts were pointless. He'd gone over and over every myth, legend and story, both spoken and written about the damnable curse.

All of this effort that Geo was putting forth was completely pointless.

There was no cure, no hope.

At one time, even his sweet Lila had tried to help him in his search for a cure, but after a few years, she had grown tired of the hunt.

She had told him it simply hurt too much to keep it up. That was when her letters had stopped, then her phone calls, save the one time a year that she allowed him to make to her.

Again, another warm tear landed in his ear, making him sit up in the bed. His pillow was drenched in salty wetness.

The phone on the nightstand caught his eye.

He mumbled in a low breath, "Should I try yet again?"

Will reached over for the phone and slowly dialed Lila's number, pausing on the last digit.

"The worst she could do is not answer", he thought as he tapped in the last number.

The phone rang for a good minute, and he started to place the receiver on its cradle when he heard an all too familiar voice answer, "Hello?"

Will jerked the receiver back to his ear, causing the phone base to wobble on the edge of the nightstand.

He went numb for just a second until he felt the light burn coming from the mark on his chest.

He cleared his throat and tried to speak, but his vocal cords were frozen stiff. The voice on the other end greeted again, this time in Romanian.

Trying once more and in perfect Romanian, Will managed to stutter out her name, "Lila...it's me."

His pulse almost halted at her silence.

She continued in her native tongue, "Hello, Will."

Her voice was distant, but not cold.

"I'm surprised you answered. It's not even November nineteenth."

He could sense her reliving the day they had met.

"I figured with that George fellow calling and trying to help our granddaughter, we probably should talk."

Tears started filling Will's eyes again, "I miss you, my love. I so want to see you again."

Will could hear her begin to cry as well, "I know, my love, but it's just not possible."

"I could borrow the amulet for a few hours. Maybe Licah would find it acceptable, so we could be together for just a while."

Taking a deep breath, Lila gently reminded Will, "You know that would not work. It would be too difficult on the both of us. Why do you wish to torture yourself and me like that, just to have to give it up all over again?"

Will pulled back his tears, "I know; it would just make it worse. But even just that small amount of time would be better than never seeing you again."

Lila began to cry harder.

Her voice reverted back to Will's native English, "No, Will! I...can't go through losing you once again. It would kill me. You know that I love you, but it hurts too much. Maybe George will find a way to help Licah, and if he does, then he can help us too."

Will's soul lightened at her words; his heart filling with hope. "I had not thought of that. Did you mail the information that Geo asked you for?"

"Yes, I just got back from doing so. It should be there in a few hours."

"Maybe he can uncover something that we never knew about, some sort of clue we missed."

Lila sighed, her hope draining away. "I hope so. That is the only way I would be comfortable with seeing you again."

Will felt his heart harden, "That is the only way?"

"Yes, my love, it is."

Lila's deadpan tone hurt Will to his core, "Then I pray Geo finds a cure. I can't live like this anymore. You are the only real thing that came into my life, and I can't even see you...your beautiful eyes. Your eyes of a goddess, and your heart of a poet are what I miss. The six months we spent together were the only time in my life that I truly lived."

Will could hear Lila's crying begin to worsen, "Will, I'm not going to get my hopes up. We have done this before, and every time we have been disappointed. I'm sorry, I must go."

"No Lila, wait!"

The other end of the line went dead before Will could get the words out of his mouth.

He threw the phone's receiver across the room and buried his head in the nearest pillow. "Why? Why do I keep doing this to myself...and to her?"

Lila was correct about the situation, but it never made it any better to hear it from her.

As Willard wept, he fell into a nightmarish sleep.

Geo awoke the next morning, his back protesting the forty dollars worth of bed.

After meeting the owners of the motel, he would not have been surprised if the room had been equipped with only a bedroll and a lantern.

The old mini-fridge hummed on the dresser across from him as he looked at his watch.

It was almost noon. He climbed off the old mattress and looked for his boots. He had slept in his clothes, just in case the need arose to leave in a fevered hurry.

After lacing his footgear, he knew it was time to talk to Saxton and then pick up the letter mailed to him by Lila.

He looked around the room to make sure he had left nothing behind and closed the door.

Geo's room was three doors down from Saxton and Licah.

He figured it was close enough to hear any room destruction ruckus without hearing any other earth moving noises that might have taken place last night.

He approached the door and lightly tapped on the faded green surface.

In less than a minute, Saxton opened the door just a crack and peered down at Geo. "Give me one second," and he closed the door.

Saxton returned and opened the door just enough to maneuver himself out and closed it back behind him. "She's sleeping. I don't want to wake her."

Geo looked at the amulet around Saxton's neck and grinned, "So, it would seem the amulet works?"

Saxton produced a large, toothy grin, which he quickly recoiled.

He didn't want to show too much excitement over last night's jaunt in their room.

He scratched at the back of his head, "Yes, it seemed to work. Otherwise, I wouldn't be standing here right now."

The answer he gave only made Geo's grin brighten. He tapped him on the shoulder and motioned him to follow, away from the motel room door.

As they crossed the damp, pothole-filled parking lot, Saxton finally spoke, "So, now that we have the amulet, we can head back to Tennessee, can't we?"

Geo shock his head, "No. This is not a cure, Saxton. If you ever take that amulet off in Licah's presence, you could quite possibly kill her."

Saxton stopped, his legs beginning to quake under his own weight, "There is no way I could ever..."

"Yes, you could Saxton. It is very possible that you could kill her, or at the very least hurt her really bad. I have to go pick up a package that should have some more information on a permanent cure for you and for her," he said, motioning toward his motel room.

Saxton looked at his feet. He spoke as he dragged his foot in the small pieces of asphalt before him, "Is this something you found out last night?"

"Yes, but I have to run. I'm sure the package is waiting on me now. Once I get back, Licah and I will go and get your truck. No use in you going down there and pissing off Willard again."

Saxton thought for a moment and finally nodded in agreement.

He followed Geo to the rented Mazda, eyeing the motel door as if waiting for Licah to step out at any time, "Where are you going to get this package?"

"The airport, I should be back in an hour. You two just hang tight until I get back."

Saxton watched him drive away, not sure what to do.

He was stuck there until Geo returned. He stared at the highway that passed near the motel. He wanted to do something to make this nightmare end, but at the moment, he just had to sit and wait.

Licah awoke feeling pleasantly sore.

She reached for Saxton only to find an empty bedside.

She pushed her long locks out of her face and squinted at the light filtering in through the curtains.

Once she was able to open her eyes, she glanced around the room to see that he wasn't there.

She wrapped the thin sheet around her and looked for a note.

Not seeing one, she walked into the bathroom to find it empty.

Her heart raced for a moment, but she suddenly knew he was okay because her mark felt normal.

She grabbed her bag and went into the bathroom.

She unwrapped the sheet from her body and looked in the mirror.

Her hair was a complete mess and she was sticky in certain...

Her mind repeated last night's events and her eyes widened, "Oh, no! We didn't use protection either time last night. What if I'm pregnant?"

She closed the bathroom door and started the shower, her thoughts continuing, "Would Saxton want a child, knowing that child would experience the same fate we have?"

She decided not to worry about it as she stepped into the tub. If she did become pregnant, she would love and cherish their child, even if he didn't.

Thoughts turned to her own father and grandfather, both of whom she had known very little, one not at all.

She wondered how her grandfather could abandon her grandmother.

Her father had died when she was young, but he had at least stuck around.

Then she remembered that the reason her grandfather disappeared was so that Anca would have a chance to have her life with her soul mate without having to worry about the curse.

At least, that was the story she had been given.

She wondered why her father had never married her mother.

Licah knew she had been born out of wedlock and given her mother's last name, not her father's.

In fact, her grandmother shared their last name, as well, and she wasn't exactly sure if Willard had ever married her grandmother.

She thought of Saxton's proposal the night before, and a smile reached her lips.

Even if she did have to pass the amulet to her daughter one day, she would take him as her husband and relish their time together.

She would not make the same mistake those before her had made.

Licah shook her head and finished rinsing off, trying to clear her mind.

Grabbing a towel, she wrapped it around her naked body and dried off.

Once her body was dry, she wrapped the towel around her wet hair and grabbed the comforter off the bed and pulled it around her.

She stepped to the door and cautiously opened it enough to see the parking lot.

Saxton was headed back to the room, his eyes fixed to the ground. He looked up and met her eyes as he approached.

"Is everything ok?" she asked as she opened the door wide for him to enter.

"Geo is going to get some more information on the curse for us. He is hoping to find a cure that will remove the curse once and for all."

Licah closed the door after Saxton entered and wrapped her arms around him. She could tell he was extremely worried about something.

"We should get ready to go soon. Geo will be back in about an hour to pick you up and go get my truck."

Licah looked up at Saxton and smiled, hinting for a kiss.

He smiled back and responding by meeting her lips with a gentleness that Licah had longed for her entire life. It was like the first kiss they had shared, all over again.

Geo arrived at the airport and searched for the package delivery station.

The place was completely packed with people. Everyone was hurriedly moving toward the terminal area, not really bothering to look around.

Finding his destination, Geo approached the counter and greeted the young man wearing a nametag reading Jay Nathan.

Geo half-smiled at him, "I need to pick up a package. It should have arrived today."

"May I see your ID please, sir?"

Taking Geo's information, Jay typed some information into his computer. "It has arrived. Give me one second to get it."

The young man disappeared into the back area while Geo looked about the airport.

He was not a fan of flying in airplanes, and the whole place made him a bit nervous.

Jay returned with the package and asked Geo to sign for it.

He scratched his name on the provided document and thanked Jay for his attention.

Package in hand, Geo quickly scurried away to the car.

He plopped into the seat and opened the package like a child on Christmas Day.

It contained several pages of old text and an old notebook. He quickly thumbed through all of them, checking to see if they could have been damaged in shipment. Satisfied it was all there and in good order, he headed back to the motel.

Licah pulled back from Saxton and said, "I need to talk to you about something."

Saxton looked at her in concern as she led him over to the bed and gestured for him to sit down.

She looked deeply into his eyes and smiled.

"Last night was absolutely amazing," she said, pleased with the grin she received in return.

"It's exactly what I've been dreaming of since the first time I saw you," he responded, taking her hands in his own and kissing her knuckles lightly.

"There is one thing," she said.

Saxton's face changed, and she could see him swallow.

"Is something wrong?" he asked, his voice growing deeper.

Licah shook her head quickly, "No, it's not that. We just didn't use protection last night, and I just wanted you to be aware that there could be a possibility of pregnancy. We should probably be more careful next time."

She had trouble reading his expression, and it took her several moments to see that it was wistfulness.

"A baby," he whispered.

Licah laughed.

"I mean, I may not be pregnant, but there's always a chance. We can stop in town and buy some con..."

Saxton rose from the bed and wrapped her in his arms, holding her close.

"I would love to have a baby with you," he whispered in her ear.

Tears formed in Licah's eyes, and she felt so relieved that he felt the same way she did.

She pulled back, and he kissed her nose, "Let's get ready before Geo comes back."

Geo pulled into the seedy motel's parking lot and stopped just in front of Saxton and Licah's room.

Seeing Geo through the window, Saxton and Licah emerged from their room.

They gave each other a parting kiss, and Licah got in the Mazda with Geo.

Geo greeted Licah with his usual smile, "Good afternoon, my dear."

Licah returned his look as she closed the car door, "Good afternoon. Did you get your package?"

Motioning to the backseat, he replied, "I did. I haven't had time to really read any of it but I figure we can all do that after we get Saxton's truck."

Pulling away from the motel, he could see Saxton waving to them.

Licah sank in her seat as they drove away.

Geo glanced at her and asked, "You okay, dear?"

"I'm fine. I just don't like leaving Saxton here. I'd rather have him with me."

"Licah, I completely understand, but it's better that he stay here and not run the risk of causing you grandfather to wolf out."

She nodded, looking straight ahead, "Let's just get Saxton's truck and get back. Then we can look over this package you received."

Geo took that as a hint that she really didn't wish to talk. He could tell that her mind was a thousand miles away.

He followed the twisted country roads and arrived on the hill above the old township.

He could see Saxton's truck in the distance, but something was horribly wrong.

Licah gasped as they approached the once pristine white F150.

Pulling the car up along side, Geo examined what was left of the truck.

All the windows were shattered and the top of the cab was peeled back like a sardine can.

Getting out of the car, he looked inside.

The seats were ripped into small fabric strips, and the steering wheel was nowhere to be seen.

Geo knew what had happened.

By the looks of things, Will had sensed Saxton's presence there earlier the day before, and his darker self had tried to take care of his enemy's possible escape.

Geo looked at Licah inside the car, "Good thing you came when you did. We would have been stranded here last night."

Licah looked almost white, "Let's just get out of here!"

It was obvious that she was scared out of her mind.

Geo sifted through the truck's remains and found what he was looking for in the passenger side floorboard.

He picked up the old volumes that Saxton had left there and brushed the glass off their covers.

Geo turned back to Licah and replied, "I found what I was looking for. Let's get you back to the motel."

Returning to his seat, he placed the recovered books in the small backseat and quickly sped away.

After returning to the motel, it was very apparent that Licah was still a little shaken up by the sight of Saxton's truck.

They stepped from the car, and Licah ran full speed and banged on the motel door, "Saxton, we are back. Please let us in."

The door quickly opened, and Licah disappeared into the room, taking Saxton with her.

Geo gathered up his books and box of papers and followed her in. He found her buried in Saxton's arms, quietly crying.

"Geo, what the hell happened?" Saxton's voice almost broke at the words.

"Son, your truck was completely ripped apart sometime yesterday. Looks as though Will didn't want us leaving."

Saxton held Licah tighter, trying to calm her tears.

The events at the church and the sight of the F150 had been more than she could handle.

"Saxton, let's get out of this place. Please! I'm so afraid you are going to be torn apart." Licah's tears matured to breathless sobs.

"It's okay baby. Geo knows what he's doing." Saxton's vision focused intently on Geo, looking for his reassurance that they would all stay safe.

"Nothing is going to happen to either of you. Just make sure you don't, under any circumstances, take off that amulet."

Saxton broke Licah's embrace and kissed her on the forehead. "Let's see what you have found."

He motioned at the small shipping box in Geo's arms.

Geo placed the four books on the nightstand and slid the contents of the package onto the edge of the bed.

There were several hand written letters, printed texts, a few photos and a small dog-eared notebook labeled *Research* across its front.

Each person in the trio picked up a small handful of the papers and tried to place them in some sort of recognizable order.

As Saxton thumbed through his small allotment, he studied one sheet of paper carefully, "Wait a second."

Geo and Licah looked up as Saxton reached to the pile of books on the nightstand and picked up the one labeled *Romanian Genealogy, 1720-1760.*

"Geo, I think we've found one of our missing pages."

Saxton rummaged through the text and arrived at page '184'. He took one of the sheets of paper from his stack and carefully laid it in place. "You see, page 185. This is the page that has all the Daciana family history listed."

Geo and Licah moved closer to the book to get a better look.

Geo's face was one of confused glee. He studied the torn page and looked at Licah with concern.

"According to this, it would appear that none of your descendants were ever married."

Licah looked at Geo, expecting some sort of judging remark.

"Don't misunderstand my statement, my dear. I'm simply saying that this would appear to be the work of the curse." He turned his attention to Saxton, "Son, were your parents married?"

Saxton looked surprised. "Well, yes. My mother has spoken of it often, even more so after Dad was killed on the job."

Geo pondered this for a couple of minutes while Saxton and Licah looked over the book.

He finally spoke, "From what I can tell from this and the research I have done in the past for Saxton, it must be your side of the family, my dear Licah, that has the need of the amulet in order to be with their true love. That would explain why your family is in possession of it."

Saxton looked at Geo in serious cluelessness, "So why didn't my side of the family need it?"

Geo began pacing the room, putting together his thoughts, "Well, there could be several reasons. First, they may not have married their true soul mate. Secondly, if they did marry their true love, there weren't enough genetic ties to the Lyall and Daciana bloodlines to cause the curse to take effect. Or thirdly, the curse only affects the Daciana soul mates. Either way, one thing is true. You both have direct lines to Romania. It would not surprise me if you both are direct descendants of the origin of this curse."

Licah looked at Geo with a confused frown, "What makes you think that?"

Geo reached for one of the other books while Saxton was still thumbing through sheets of paper.

He opened the book and turned to the section about the Werewolf's curse, "You see here, Licah, it tells the details of the curse. However, there is a page missing from this book as well, and I bet that page has the information to prove my theory."

Saxton's hand shot up, paper between his fingers, "You mean this page?"

Geo took the sheet from him and studied it closely.

His eyes widened slightly, "Yes! This is it."

On the sheet, it listed all the direct descendants from the nineteen thirties all the way back to the early seventeen hundreds. From nineteen thirty to present day had been penciled in.

There, in black and white, was mapped out how Saxton and Licah's heritage went back to Dak Lyall and Yeaserna Daciana.

Saxton and Liach looked at each other, mouths wide in astonishment.

She studied the text given to her by Geo very closely, but quickly said, "So you are saying that I am directly related to the lady that started the curse in the first place?"

Geo's face hardened, "Correct, but now since we have this information, maybe we can find a way to reverse it. Let's get this in order and see what we can find in common with every member of your two families.

Chapter Eleven

Saxton sat, blurry eyed, looking through the books that he had brought from Tennessee. He didn't think he could read another sentence without passing out.

Licah lay curled up behind him on the bed, her back resting against his. She had fallen asleep about an hour earlier.

Geo, on the other hand, looked like his same old chipper self.

Saxton could hear him occasionally humming a song not familiar to him.

He was eating up every scrap of knowledge he could put his eyes to. He had nearly completed reading the old notebook.

Saxton looked at him and yawned, "We have been at this for six hours, and I know no more now than I did then, other than, a bunch of names of family members that have been dead a couple centuries."

Finishing off the notebook, Geo closed it with a dusty snap. "I have an idea on what we need to do, but we need to get back to Memphis, so I can look over some previous research."

248

Saxton looked at his friend with utmost seriousness, "You think you have found a cure?"

Geo put his hand up in protest, "Now, I didn't say that, son. I need to look over some things before I can comment to anything. If my suspicions are correct, this is gonna have to be something that we do very soon."

Saxton took in another breath to ask why time played a factor in it, but decided against it.

He had seen Geo when he'd been asked too many questions, and it was something he did not wish to repeat.

Geo began gathering up the books and papers, preparing to leave.

"We should go. Wake Licah up, and let her know we are headed back to Memphis."

The three arrived at the Bangor airport and Geo was fit to be tied.

He hadn't taken into account they would have to leave the rental car in Maine. Since Saxton's truck was demolished, the only choice was to fly.

Licah and Saxton had volunteered to pay half the price of Geo's ticket back to Memphis, but that still had not appeased him.

He sat with his arms crossed like a child that was about to have a temper tantrum, "You aren't getting me on a plane. Back in my day, you didn't trust any manmade contraption with your life. It's like flying in a giant beer can."

Licah and Saxton looked at each other as Geo pulled into the airport.

Licah spoke up. "It's the only way we can get you back home. The cost of the rental would be several times that of a plane ticket. Plus, you told Saxton yourself, that if there is a cure for breaking this curse, it could be a time sensitive matter."

Saxton had never seen Geo act so strange, and that was saying something.

The man never showed fear of anything. The idea of flying, however, had him tied in a knot.

"Geo please, we need you to do this. It will make our trip home so much faster."

Stopping the car, Geo jumped out, his face red with anger.

He picked up his stack of belongings and slammed the door, "Fine, but if I get killed up there, be forewarned, I will haunt you two for the rest of your lives."

Saxton and Licah got out on the other side and walked around to Geo, who tossed the keys to her and headed for the terminal.

Licah turned to Saxton, her eyes wide, "What's the matter with him?"

Saxton shrugged, "I have no idea. I have never seen him like this. I guess he really hates the thought of flying."

The two walked to the desk to return the keys from the rental car.

The same unfortunate fellow who had given the keys to Licah the first time was on duty again and on his cell phone.

The man started to back away as Licah approached. "I...gotta go," he said into the phone and quickly turned it off.

Licah smirked at him and set the keys on the counter, "Do I need to sign anything?"

He looked as though he were about to urinate on himself.

He stammered for a moment, "No...you're good. Thank you for returning the keys."

He quickly pulled the keys to him and retreated into the back room.

Saxton noticed the young man's demeanor, "What's eating him?"

Licah laughed, "I got eyes for him, that's all."

Saxton looked at her, concerned. "What do you mean?"

251

She took him by the arm and cuddled him lovingly as they walked through the terminal, "It's a long story. I will tell you on the flight."

Spotting Geo, they got in line to buy three tickets to Memphis.

Hours later, Saxton and Licah watched as Geo kissed the pavement outside the Memphis International Airport.

The flight had been an absolute nightmare for the man.

He'd spent the entire flight in the aisle seat, complaining profusely if anyone dared try opening their window shades within three rows in each direction.

He'd held onto his armrests with white knuckles, refusing to engage in conversation with Licah or Saxton.

On take-off and landing, Licah swore he had turned positively green.

So they allowed him his personal time with the ground, they just hoped he wouldn't spend all day.

Geo's stomach finally started to settle down, and he blessed every deity he knew of, which was an extensive list, for their safe landing.

He took a few deep breaths and looked up to see he had drawn a crowd of gawkers.

He blushed and looked up to Licah and Saxton, who stood nearby, staring at him with smirks on their faces.

"I'm sorry," he said, grabbing his things from the pavement and standing up with what little dignity he had left.

They went to Licah's jeep and climbed in, Licah at the wheel.

Knowing that Geo was still a little shaky from his flight experience, Saxton climbed in the back, letting Geo have the front seat.

Geo protested at first, but when he saw Saxton leaning forward to snuggle Licah while she drove, he didn't feel so badly.

"So, what now?" Saxton asked, running his hands through Licah's long hair.

Licah muttered under her breath, but kept her hands on the wheel.

"I think that you two need to go back to the cabins and resume life as usual. Once I've analyzed all this again, I'll contact you, and we'll figure out what to do. I have to be alone," he glanced at Licah's hooded eyes as Saxton continued to stroke her neck and hair, "and I believe you two do, too."

After dropping Geo off at his bookshop, Saxton and Licah arrived at Stone Creek Park as the sun was going down.

"Do you need to go home?" she asked, halting at the stop sign where they had to turn to go to either cabin.

"Just for a minute, so I can grab a few things," he said, looking at her with pure lust, "Then we'll go back to your place. I have an idea of how we can pass the time until Geo calls."

A shiver ran up Licah's spine when she met his gaze and nodded.

Her hands shook as she turned the wheel and shifted into second, then third, to creep up to his cabin.

When they pulled into his drive, the plywood board nailed over the hole where the large picture window used to be sobered them both.

"I can't imagine how I would have lived with myself if I had hurt you that night," Saxton whispered.

Licah reached over and took his hand.

He pulled her hand to his lips and kissed her knuckles very gently.

He looked into her eyes and said, "I love you so much. I'm so glad you had this amulet."

Licah smiled and said, "Go get your things, I'll wait here."

Saxton nodded and climbed out of the jeep.

He hated leaving Licah for even a second, so he rushed into the cabin and grabbed a change of clothes and his toothbrush.

He was almost out the door when he noticed a paper lying on his recently replaced kitchen table.

Someone had cleaned up the wreckage in the dining room, also.

He grabbed the note and unfolded it.

Sax,

This is the bill for the repairs and the table. Since you've offered no explanation for what happened, the Parker's Ridge City Council is billing you for the damage.

It's funny to me that you've been acting weird since that Daciana chick moved in. What's wrong with you? Yeah, she's a famous author, but she'll be gone soon.

Then what are you going to do?

Sam

Saxton grabbed the bill for six hundred dollars, stuffed it in his pocket and then tossed the note in the garbage.

He had more things to worry about than a job and a horny intern.

Licah watched Saxton leave his cabin and hurry toward the jeep. When he climbed in, he had an odd look on his face.

"What's wrong?"

He smiled at her and shook his head.

"Nothing that can't wait."

She looked at him for a moment and then nodded. She wasn't going to push. They were under enough stress without starting a fight.

She pulled out of the driveway and turned toward the other side of the park.

As she passed by one cabin, Saxton put his hand on her arm.

She glanced at him with a question in her gaze.

"Slow down," he said, peering over her shoulder.

She slowed and saw the smoking girl standing on the porch of the cabin in a heavy lip-lock with none other than Jackson, the mechanic.

Licah laughed out loud and drove a little faster.

Saxton looked at her curiously.

"He was just hitting on me a few days ago," she said with mirth.

She was looking back at the road when she heard a growl trickle from her right.

She hit the brakes and looked at Saxton with fear in her eyes.

But, it was just Saxton. He was still staring at the couple who were now looking in their direction.

"What?" she asked irritatingly.

He shook his head trying to snap out of it.

"I'm sorry. It was just a reaction."

Licah cocked her head and laughed.

"Am I your territory or something?" she asked jovially.

Saxton was taken aback, and then his forehead crinkled, pondering what he'd just done.

"I think its part of the curse. I know you're not my territory; I mean, I don't plan on pissing on you or anything," he laughed, "But I think the reason I survived that attack with your grandfather was because you were there for me to protect. And now, I know that Jackson was trying to put the moves on you and that growl just came out of nowhere. I know it sounds barbaric, but, yes, I guess you are."

Licah palmed his cheek and ran her thumb over his bottom lip.

"I've always been yours, Saxton. Nothing's going to change that, especially now."

Geo sat at his desk; notebooks, books, and papers spread before him.

He knew that what he was thinking was definitely a long shot, but it made so much sense.

If, on the anniversary of the curse, Saxton and Licah married in the old Romanian custom in the same place where the curse was laid, he thought it was possible that the curse might be lifted.

And the fact that this September thirtieth was a full moon didn't hurt.

He glanced at a calendar. It was September twenty-seventh. Three days.

If this were truly the cure, they had three days to figure out the ceremony and get to Romania.

He took off his glasses and rubbed his eyes.

It was such a small chance, but he thought it just might work.

He picked up the phone and started to dial Saxton when he realized one uninterrupted night with Licah would lift the man's spirits so much.

Instead, he dialed Willard.

"Hello?" Willard slurred into the phone.

"Willard, it's Geo."

Willard started to laugh under his breath.

"What do you want you vechi ticălos?"

Geo knew better than to take offense to being called an old bastard in Romanian. He knew Willard had been drinking.

"I need to ask you something."

Willard sighed.

"Don't you think that you have plunged the knife into my heart as far as it will go?" he asked roughly.

Geo took the plunge.

"Why did you never marry Lila?"

Geo braced himself for a dial tone or a crash, but oddly enough, he just heard Willard whimper.

"Do you have any idea what it's like to know that you have hurt the one you love when you don't even remember doing it?" he asked softly.

Guilt ran through Geo, and he closed his eyes at the memories flooding through him.

"Yes, I do know."

Willard laughed brokenheartedly.

"You know what? I believe you. You have never lied to me prietenul meu. But you've never told me the truth either. You know what I am, tell me what you are, and I will tell you everything you need to know."

Geo took a deep breath at Will calling him 'my friend' and looked into a mirror across from his desk.

He kept it there to remind himself of the glamour he had to keep around himself at all times.

He had kept it for so long; it was like breathing to maintain.

"I am a feeric," he replied with the Romanian word for faery.

He waited for a retort and heard Willard start to chuckle. His chuckle turned into a laugh. And his laugh turned into a guffaw.

"You mean to tell me that my old friend is one of the wee folk?"

Geo smiled at the Irish term.

It was amazing how the man had adopted not only his mate's Romanian terms and an American southern accent, but had maintained some of his own culture as well.

"Yes. You are the only one I have told that is currently living," he admitted, "in the old country they called me the Bailitheoir Scéalta, loosely translated as the Collector of Stories."

Willard laughed again, "Very fitting. Now I know why you stay in that dusty old bookstore all the time. But you have left it to help my kin, why?"

Geo laughed.

"I said stories, not just books. Stories are collected in more than just pages. Sometimes experiencing your own stories is far better than any you could read."

"Fine. I didn't marry my mate because she wouldn't let me. None of the Daciana women have ever married one of their mates because of the curse. I asked Lila once why that was, and she said that each had made a pact with their mothers and grandmothers before them that they would never marry."

Geo frowned.

"Why is that?" he asked.

Willard's voice was deadly calm when he said, "I'm going to answer this, and then, I don't want you to call me again. Take care of Licah; do what you have to do, but I don't want to ever hear from you again."

Geo understood his friend's demand.

"I can promise that I will not call you," he answered.

One thing about the Fae most people didn't know these days, they can't lie. But, the most important thing about that was, they were very good at dancing around the truth, while still furthering their own ends.

"She told me none of them would tie their mates down to marriage, knowing they would have to pass the amulet on as soon as one of their daughters came of age. Because once the amulet was passed on, they would abandon their mates for their children and never see them again."

Geo heard the dial tone come down the line, he found it was bittersweet that he had promised his friend that he wouldn't call again. But it didn't mean Saxton and Licah couldn't.

Licah walked into the bedroom and heard when Saxton shut the bathroom door.

She tiptoed quickly as she could to her closet and rummaged through a bag to find the slinkiest black teddy she owned.

She quickly stripped off her clothing, throwing them into the bottom of the closet, and slipped on the teddy.

She brushed her hair, sprayed on some perfume, and turned down the thick comforter.

After propping the pillows up against the headboard, she got on the bed and leaned against them, assuming an alluring pose.

When Saxton came out of the bathroom in nothing but an unbuttoned pair of jeans, he stopped cold in the doorway, drinking her in with his eyes.

"I don't think I've ever seen anything more sexy or beautiful in my life," he said barely above a whisper.

He kept his eyes locked on hers as he approached the bed and crawled over the end in an almost predatory manner.

He reached for her foot and Licah watched him kneel down and kiss every toe and then move to her other foot.

Swapping to her ankles, he nibbled them and kissed his way up to her knee.

His tongue shot out, and he licked the back of her knee in a spot that made her gasp.

He continued to lick that spot until she had wadded the bed sheet up in her hands.

She'd never known such an ordinary spot could set her on fire.

Saxton finally relented only to nibble up her thigh to her hip.

He tested her hipbone with his teeth and then lapped over it quickly, causing her to writhe again.

He sat back and ran his finger along the edge of black lace covering her mons.

Licah desperately ached for him to touch her, but he continued tracing the lace until he came to her side. He ran his nails around her waist as she watched his hands' movements.

His eyes fixated on her breasts, barely visible through the floral pattern of the lace, and he ran his thumb over her puckered nipples.

He reached for her delicate hand and took her fingers one by one into his mouth, running his tongue softly over each.

He took her wrist and bit her pulse point, which hammered against his teeth.

She couldn't take it anymore, she reached behind his neck and roughly pulled his mouth to hers, and Saxton burst in action.

The delicate piece of material was shredded in seconds, and Saxton's jeans hit the floor.

He pulled her onto his lap and plunged deep inside her while sitting up on the bed.

Licah propped up on her knees and rode him until her body exploded only to hear Saxton exclaim as she felt him spill his seed inside her.

They both stopped all movement and caught their breath for a moment.

Saxton rubbed her back softly as she sat in his lap with her head on his shoulder.

Saxton turned his head and nibbled her neck. She tensed just briefly when she felt him grow hard inside her again.

She looked at him oddly, and he laughed, causing strange sensations to run through her lower body.

"That was just the appetizer."

Chapter Twelve

Geo jerked awake to the echo of a loud clambering.

He looked around to find the source of the disturbance and saw the pile of books on the floor that he had apparently knocked off the desk.

The dust from the old texts still lingered in the air.

He straightened in his chair and realized he had fallen asleep at his desk...again.

It happened a lot.

He went to rub his eyes and found a large sticky note on his cheek. He peeled it off and placed it in front of him.

Geo had been up most of the night researching, digging, and analyzing a small portion of Willard's books.

His main objective was to find any information on Romanian marriage rites from roughly three hundred years ago.

There before him, written on a five by seven note card, was at least one version of the ceremony that needed to be performed.

He folded it and placed it in his pocket for safekeeping.

Finding that, he knew he would have to compare it to other rituals from that era.

He knew the next step was finding the location of the wedding that had taken place in Romania, around the year seventeen forty-two.

Geo acknowledged the clock was quickly ticking the hours away, and it was time to enlist some more eyes to get the task at hand completed before the sun rose on September thirtieth.

He had forty-eight hours to find the needed location in Romania and get Saxton and Licah there to complete the correct ceremony and end the dreaded curse that had followed their families for so long.

Geo rose from his desk and headed for his telephone, his back stiff from sleeping over the top of his antique desk.

Recalling that Saxton's cell phone had been smashed to pieces in Maine, he decided to call Licah's.

He knew he was going to be interrupting something, but it really didn't matter in the grand scheme of things.

There was very little time.

He dialed the number and waited for Licah's sweet voice to pick up. After an uncountable number of rings, Geo finally heard, "Hello?"

Geo cut straight to the point, "Licah, I think I may have this figured out, but I need you and Saxton back here in Memphis, pronto. We have two days to find a certain location in Romania and get you two married."

Licah nearly dropped the phone, "Married? Is that going to break the curse?"

"There's more to it than that, but I don't have time to explain. You and Saxton meet me here at the bookstore. Licah, I seriously need you to hurry."

Licah's voice was calm yet professional, "I understand. We will be there soon."

The line went dead, and Geo replaced the receiver into the phone's cradle.

Returning to his desk, Geo's eyes shimmered with excitement, "Now, back to the task at hand."

The morning sun reflected off of Licah's rented jeep as she pulled into the front of The Mystics' Book Emporium.

Saxton had had the entire trip to ponder the news that Licah had received over the phone, and after she put the jeep in park, he reached over, took her hand, and looked into her eyes.

His feelings bubbled to the surface, "Licah, I just want you to know that whatever happens, I will not let anything happen to you. I will keep you safe, one way or another."

He sat tightly gripping the amulet hanging from his neck with his free hand.

Licah could tell he was squeezing the metal disk with all his strength, "You just keep that amulet around your neck and everything will be fine. Now, let's go inside."

He leaned forward to kiss her, and she responded by meeting him half way. Not wanting to stop, but knowing she had to, Licah pulled away and patted him on the knee, "Come on, baby. Let's see what Geo has found out."

They both exited the jeep and met at the front of it to take each other's hand.

Saxton inquired, "You've never been here before have you?"

She shook her head, "No, but I remember Jessica speaking of it a few times back in high school."

Saxton smiled as he muscled the door open for her, "You being a writer, I have a feeling you are going to love this place."

The usual sounds and smells of the bookshop engulfed Licah while Saxton watched her reaction.

He could tell she was not disappointed.

She spun around a couple of times, taking in the scenery, her mouth opening slightly, "This place is amazing!"

Suddenly, Geo popped out from one of the back rooms, his facial expression stern and focused, "Good, you're here."

Stopping mid-stride, he motioned them in his direction. "Follow me into the back."

Licah looked at Saxton, concern filling her eyes.

He patted her hand and softly whispered, "It's fine, sweetie. Geo's a great man."

Geo had turned around and was already heading back into the room. A smile crossed his lips as he heard Saxton's words to Licah.

His hearing was very acute, and he missed very little of what people said around him. That is, unless he wanted to.

Saxton and Licah entered the back room. It was the same room he had dug through just a few days before.

Licah's eyes widened at the scene.

Geo had placed seven timeworn books in a row on a large table that lined the back wall.

Each book had been left open to a specific page and open tablets sat between each volume.

Three chairs were set up at the long table, and Geo motioned for them to sit.

"Okay, here is what we must do to get this curse wiped out for good."

Geo pointed at the books on the table, "These are all the books I own about Romanian custom. Each of these books cover various wedding ceremonies. With the notebooks I have provided, the two of you need to transcribe the seven rituals and have them ready for when we go to Romania."

Saxton's eye nearly bugged out of his head, "Romania!"

His arms crossed, Geo looked at Licah with a disagreeable smirk.

She turned to look at Saxton, shrugging her shoulders "Yeah, did I forget to mention that part?"

Saxton almost laughed, but knew that Geo was not amused.

Geo cleared his throat and pointed at an eighth book that he had sat aside, "I will be finishing up what location we will be headed to once we are there."

Licah looked at Geo and almost raised her hand for permission to speak, "Umm...couldn't we just use a copying machine to have copies of the different rituals?"

Geo face drew a very sour scowl.

He answered back in a somewhat mocking tone, "No, we can't use a copying machine to have copies of the different rituals. It doesn't work that way. You two have to do it. Once you have, I can marry up the versions in route to Romania and have the completed rite."

Licah started to lash back at his attitude, but thought better of it. "I see," was all she said.

"Licah, once I figure out where we are going in Romania, I need you to make the travel arrangements for a rental vehicle when we arrive," his voice trailed off for a moment, "and for the flight over there."

Saxton laughed at seeing him so uncomfortable talking about flying.

Geo walked to his singular book and opened it, "Let's get to work people. Time's a wasting."

"We're getting married in Transylvania?" Saxton exclaimed, jumping from his chair, the chair clattering to the floor.

Geo palmed his face and shook his head.

"Boy, will you sit down?"

Saxton tried not to take offense at being called a boy, while he repositioned his chair next to Licah and took her hand.

He could tell that she was trying desperately not to laugh, and that lifted his spirits.

"Allow me to give you a little geography lesson. Transylvania is a region of the Carpathian Mountains in Romania. There is a city in the mountains called Sibiu. Just south of Sibiu is where the Transylvanian region turns into the Wallachian region. On this border is where the original curse took place in a small village called Cisnădioara. This is where the original curse took place in seventeen forty-two."

Licah looked at Geo strangely.

"My grandmother told me she thought it took place in Wallachia."

Geo nodded.

"I can see where the misunderstanding would be easy. Your family was the Roma. Gypsies. They travelled from town to town with abandon, looking for work or villages to sell their wares. It wouldn't be hard to confuse the two, as back then, the lines were not clearly drawn. Who is to say that Cisnădioara was not a part of Wallachia back then?"

Licah nodded her understanding.

She had always known she was of gypsy heritage. They had even called her gypsy girl in high school. Her mother and grandmother still practiced the arts. But she'd never had it so in her face before.

Licah pulled out her cell phone and began looking at flights.

"Uh, guys. We've got to go now."

Geo and Saxton looked up from their books with worry on their faces.

"The next flight leaves in an hour, and it takes eighteen hours to get to Bucharest. Once we're there, it'll take us three hours of busting tail to get to Cisnădioara."

Saxton, at Geo's insistence, rang Willard's phone for the third time while Geo drove the jeep, and Licah talked to her grandmother.

He waited for the answering machine to pick up again, but suddenly the ringing stopped, and he heard breathing on the other end.

"This better not be you, Geo."

Saxton felt a growl creep up his throat, but he tamped it down and said, "No, it's not Geo, old man. It's Saxton, Licah's mate."

Saxton heard a return growl.

"What do you want, pup?"

Saxton stiffened his spine and took a deep breath and repeated a mantra inside his head, "I am not a beast, I am a man, I am not a beast, I am a man."

He began matter of factly, "I need you on a flight to Bucharest as fast as inhumanly possible. We've found a cure, but we're down to the wire on time. You've got to be in Cisnădioara, Romania on September thirtieth, to break this curse."

Willard stopped growling.

"What do you mean?" he asked gruffly.

"It's so simple. We have to marry our mates, Willard. It's how we break the curse. But we have to do it on the anniversary of the curse in the same location the curse was laid."

Licah and Geo, bless them, had written down instructions and a flight schedule for Willard.

"Get a pen, write this down."

The flight from Memphis to Chicago had only taken two hours, but they were stuck with a three hour layover and the clock was ticking.

Geo had done a lot better with the last flight, his eyes abnormally bright with the excitement.

Licah fidgeted while they ate breakfast in the airport cafeteria.

Her coffee felt as though it was curdling in her stomach as she looked at Saxton with longing.

What if it didn't work? What if when Willard showed up, they would kill each other? What if... What if... What if...

Saxton looked up from his pancakes and stopped chewing.

He reached down, took her hand, and held it to the mark on his chest.

"Stop. We're doing what we can. If we have to wait another year, it will be fine. As long as I'm with you, nothing else matters."

Licah seemed to shrink in her seat at his words.

He was right. What was another year to a lifetime?

Her cell phone rang, and her grandmother's heavily accented voice passed over the receiver.

"We're on our way. Have you spoken to Willard?"

Licah nodded, and then realized she couldn't see her.

"Yes, Saxton spoke to him. He's been given the information he needs."

Her grandmother paused for several moments before speaking again.

"I know you are thinking the same thing I am thinking, Licah. How can they be in the same place at the same time without killing each other?"

Licah closed her eyes.

Who would have thought, after all these years, that Licah and her grandmother would be bound together by such circumstances?

"We'll figure it out. We have to have hope."

They said their goodbyes and she turned to Saxton and Geo.

"They're on their way."

Willard hadn't flown in years, and he felt memories flood through him.

He and Lila had flown so many times to so many places in their short time together.

Being a commander in the service, he had refused to leave her behind.

He closed his eyes and remembered her vivid green eyes and her long black hair that she always braided down her back.

He remembered the flowing colorful skirts and scarves she wore, seeming like an Irish faery come to life.

Her movements were always so fluid, and yet calculated.

Her eyes were always full of cunning, and she rarely missed anything, even if she never spoke of it.

A wave of emotion flooded his heart, and he rubbed his old paw mark on his chest.

Would she really want to marry him, knowing that he had hurt her?

Would she really show up in Romania or was he taking a flight to his doom?

He was too old for this.

That brought a new wave of emotion.

He looked at his reflection in the airplane window and saw his wrinkled visage and gray-shot black hair.

Would she still want him?

Anca sat next to her mother on the plane and tried desperately not to think of Robert.

Not a single day had passed since his death, that he wasn't on her mind.

She hoped this plan of Licah's worked. She would hate for her mother and her daughter to feel the emptiness that plagued her.

She reached over and took her mother's weathered hand in her own, smiling at the five inch line of bracelets clinking on her wrist.

This was it.

If Licah's plan didn't work, the Daciana line may well die with the curse.

Saxton brushed his hand through Licah's hair as they sat on the plane from Chicago to Warsaw.

He'd never been across the pond.

In another time, he would've been ill that he wouldn't get time to sightsee, but time was of the essence, and if the plan worked, they would have plenty of time to see whatever he wanted.

He looked at her closed eyelids and traced his finger over her thin eyebrows.

He couldn't lose her.

If he lost her, he didn't think he could live.

He looked over to Geo and noticed he was watching him.

"What?" he asked the older man.

Geo shook his head.

"Such love is the stuff of legends. I find myself very blessed to witness it."

Saxton smiled and blushed.

"You've loved her all these years and never knew her. Now that you are together, it's like the whole world has come back together."

Saxton nodded.

"I feel complete with her. I never knew I was walking around so empty until I was finally able to touch and be with her."

Geo smiled and leaned his head back against the headrest of his plane seat.

He was pleased that he had adapted to flying fairly quickly.

His stomach didn't feel as if it were going to crawl out his of mouth anymore.

He let his mind wander to another time and another place, to a face he hadn't thought of in years.

Salwera.

Her eyes were like iridescent mirrors.

Her skin sparkled like sugar in the sun.

Her wings were so thin, yet so strong as she had fluttered around the Court.

He heard a gasp and looked up to see Saxton looking at him strangely.

Had he dropped his glamour?

"Are you okay?" he asked, trying to be nonchalant.

Saxton nodded, but continued to look at him like something happened.

Geo decided it wasn't worth the effort. If he had dropped his glamour, Saxton would ask him about it in his own time.

The layover from Warsaw to Bucharest had only been an hour, and once they finally stood on Romanian soil, they all took a collective breath.

Licah wandered over to the service desk and said, "Am nevoie de o masina."

The young man smiled at her flirtatiously, and she heard Saxton growl behind her.

"I just told him we needed a car," she said, turning to her mate and meeting his gaze.

She felt her mark pulse, and she squeezed his hand.

"Un utilitar sport vehicul, dacă este posibil," she told the young man.

They would need a large vehicle if they all met up as planned.

It felt so strange using Romanian again. She usually only spoke it with her grandmother, because, especially in her own home, Lila refused to use English.

She passed the young man her credit card and waited while he retrieved keys.

"Vă mulțumim pentru afacerea ta," he thanked her as he passed the card and keys back.

Licah nodded and picked up her bag and grabbed Saxton's hand.

"I wonder if you're going to be this jealous once the wolf is gone," she asked with a smirk.

Saxton smiled sheepishly at her while thinking how to properly decapitate the young man at the counter.

The trip through the Meridional Carpathian Mountains seemed to take forever to Licah.

She was so ready for this to be over.

She worried about what would happen that night when they reached the curse site.

Geo drove, seeming perfectly at ease at the wheel in a foreign country.

They reached Cisnădioara, Romania at five o'clock in the afternoon just as the sun began to descend the horizon.

Licah called her mother, hoping the one bar on her cell phone would be enough to reach wherever they were.

"Da?" he grandmother answered.

"Where are you?" she asked, glancing up at an ancient fortified church making up the town square.

Its yellowing walls and sloped reddish-brown roofs were distinctly Romanian.

"Your mother is driving, we are outside Cisnădioara. Meet us at Cisnădie."

Licah looked puzzled for a moment. Surely her grandmother knew better than to assume she knew of some obscure part of the township.

"Licah, it's the church in the middle of the village. You can't miss it."

She smiled as she looked up at the church and said, "You're right, we're already here."

Anca departed the taxi and paid the driver two hundred and sixty lei. Roughly twenty-five dollars.

She helped her mother out of the car and looked up to see Licah running toward them, a young red-headed man and an older, shorter man lagging behind.

She caught her daughter in her arms and squeezed her tight.

"Draga mea dragoste," she whispered "my dearest love" into her daughter's black, silky locks.

Licah pulled back and looked at her grandmother, the mark on her chest began to burn, but in a way she had never felt before.

Grief and fear bathed Licah as she took her grandmother into her arms.

"Indiferent de ceea ce se întâmplă, nul lăsa decolare amuleta," she whispered, taking Licah's face in her old weathered hands.

Licah looked at her strangely.

"But grandmother, if he doesn't take off the amulet, how will we know it worked?"

Lila stepped back and brushed her hair away from her neck, showing old white scars Licah had never seen before.

"Willard şi voi decide că."

Tears stung her eyes at her grandmother's offer.

"What did she say?" Saxton asked, who had been watching the exchange.

Licah turned to him and said, "She said whatever you do, don't take off the amulet. That she and Willard will decide if the curse is lifted.

Saxton reached up to Lila's neck and traced the old scars, watching the old woman's reaction.

As his skin touched hers, she closed her eyes.

"It has been so long since I was touched by a male with the mark," Lila whispered, taking Saxton's hand and moving it away.

Licah looked at Saxton strangely.

"How are you reacting to her?" she asked, hoping for an answer she could deal with.

Saxton looked to Licah with a grin.

"Jealous?" he asked.

Licah hit him with her shoulder bag and grinned.

"Have no fear, my love. I feel only protective of Lila and Anca."

Anca, who had been watching the exchange next to Geo, said, "Only the one who caused the mark to burn will ever turn that one's head. Have no fear, Licah. We will not steal your man away."

They all laughed and Saxton took Licah into his arms.

Geo stepped up, "Time is running out."

Willard drove up the mountain in a rickety little two door. He thought if he made it to Cisnădioara with his bones still attached, it would be a miracle.

His mind went back to Lila.

Sweet Lila.

Without the amulet, Will knew he would be a danger to everyone who had made their trek across the ocean.

His plan was simple, stay hidden away until the curse had been lifted from Saxton and to use the amulet himself.

He prayed a silent prayer that no harm would come to anyone, but especially his long lost love, his daughter, and his granddaughter.

The biggest problem at the moment seemed to be in finding the rest of the group without getting too close.

Will had no intention of causing the curse to react.

He had no cell phone. Never had a reason to need one, but one would've come in very handy right then.

He decided his best course of action would be to follow the slight burn of his mark until it got just on the good side of unbearable.

Will chuckled to himself. The first joyful laugh he'd made in years, "Lila radar."

Geo pulled the Grand Cherokee onto a large plateau in the mountains.

He could feel the tell-tale signs of an unworldly presence about the area in which they had arrived.

He maneuvered the SUV to the center of the highland and stopped for everyone to get out. He thought to himself, "What a motley crew I have in here with me. A country park ranger, a famous writer, her mother, and a lady that probably shares some similar memories with me from a time long dead."

Saxton slid out of one of the back doors, followed by Licah.

Anca followed suit on the other side and went to open the front passenger door to help her aging mother out.

Geo stared momentarily across the landscape, listening intently.

His hands were tightly fixed to the vehicle's steering wheel. He was the first to speak, "This has got to be the place."

Upon exiting, Geo took in a deep gulp of the mountain air.

It filled his lungs and lifted his spirits a bit higher.

He looked at Saxton and displayed his usual grin, "We should get started."

Geo walked to the back hatch of the SUV and opened it.

The sound of the door's hydraulics echoed around the deserted plateau.

The area was completely boxed in by high cliffs or near bottomless valleys, save the path they had taken and another going higher up the steep mountain.

Saxton and Licah stood next to him as he dug into one of the large bags he had brought for the trip.

He pulled out a small oil lantern for everyone and passed them out. "Try not to use these too much. I only have enough fuel to refill each of them once."

Licah looked at him, questioning his approach, "Why didn't you just bring flashlights?"

Geo looked at her, then handed over a lantern. His face tightened at her question, but he said nothing.

She smiled back at him, batting her beautiful green eyes, "Let me guess, it doesn't work that way, right?"

He laughed loud enough that it echoed all across the plateau, "Right!"

Saxton saw the glee in Geo's eyes at all of this.

Something he had seen in the past, but not with that much enthusiasm.

It was obvious this was something he lived for, but at the same time, he knew what was at stake.

Lighting Lila and Anca's lanterns, Saxton returned to the back of the jeep.

Opening the zipper on another bag, Geo pulled out a notebook that had, he hoped, the correct version of the wedding ceremony. He knew to guard it carefully. Without it, they could do the rites in the wrong order.

"You two have your parts memorized?"

Licah answered, "We worked pretty hard on it on the plane."

Geo eyed Saxton, "Can you pronounce the words correctly?

289

Saxton shifted his feet, afraid to answer, "God, I hope so. I have been told I can barely speak English."

To change the subject he questioned the notebook in Geo's hand, "Who's gonna do the ceremony?"

Geo started to laugh, but realized that in their haste to get there, he had not shared that information with them.

"Oh, I will be performing the ceremony."

Licah's grandmother started to protest in Romanian.

Saxton's eyes grew large at how such a small woman could carry so much volume.

He smiled at Licah nervously, wondering if she were of the same caliber.

Licah could read his expression, "Not to worry baby, we will always make up afterwards."

She wrapped her arms around his waist.

Geo waved his hands at Lila to explain, "It's fine, it's fine, Ms. Daciana. I am completely ordained."

Saxton looked at his friend in disbelief, "Since when?"

Geo wasn't sure what answer to give, "Longer than you have been alive, son."

Saxton's old friend never ceased to amaze him.

He had learned a long time ago there was no way he would ever know everything about him.

"So, what's our next move?"

Anca interrupted, "What about my dad? He isn't here yet."

Geo tried to reassure her, "He should be here soon. I'm hoping he will get here after we have completed the ritual."

Licah's complexion turned pale.

She knew why, as surely as they all knew.

If her grandfather got there too early, Saxton would be ripped to pieces.

She held onto him tighter, causing him to look down into her emerald eyes and begin to kiss her.

Geo looked at the two of them, "Okay, you two. You're gonna have to put the brakes on for a while. We are running out of time. Let's get started."

Chapter Thirteen

Geo stood before Licah and Saxton on a particularly powerful spot Geo had chosen.

He had asked Anca to stand behind Saxton to translate, as the rite had to be done in Romanian.

"Ne-am adunat astăzi aici pentru a uni acest cuplu de tineri în căsătorie. Licah Daciana şi Saxton Lyall, nu vă luaţi fiecare alt organism, inima, şi sufletul?" Geo read from his notebook.

Anca translated, "We are gathered here today to unite this young couple in marriage. Licah Daciana and Saxton Lyall, do you take each other body, heart, and soul?"

They both replied, "Da."

Geo pulled a knife out of his pocket and handed it to Saxton.

Saxton looked into Licah's eyes as he pierced the flesh of his left hand with the tip of the dagger.

He prayed he would pronounce the next part right.

"Sângele meu, sânge, sânge nostru ne combina pentru toată veşnicia."

Anca whispered the translation, "My blood, your blood, our blood combines us for all eternity."

He handed the dagger to Licah and she repeated the words as she pierced the flesh of her right hand.

Geo took a small silver chalice from Lila and a white cloth.

He first held the chalice under Saxton's hand, catching the blood. Then to Licah, catching hers.

He then handed the chalice back to Lila, and took the white silky cloth in his right hand.

"Acum, o iei de mana miresei dumneavoastră, Saxton Lyall, combina sânge."

Anca whispered, "Now, take your bride's hand, Saxton Lyall, combine your blood."

Saxton took Licah's right hand and placed his cut carefully over hers, making sure to line them up so that their blood intermingled.

"Licah Daciana, vei fi sânge din sângele meu? Carne din carnea mea? Vei fi soția mea?" Saxton asked with tears in his eyes.

He nearly gasped, his mark pulsating forcefully.

Licah wavered as Anca translated.

"Licah Daciana, will you be blood of my blood? Flesh of my flesh? Will you be my wife?"

"Da."

Licah then squeezed Saxton's hand.

"Saxton Lyall, vei fi sânge din sângele meu? Carne din carnea mea? Vei fi soția mea?"

"Da," Saxton replied.

Geo turned to Lila, who had tears streaming down the wrinkles of her face.

He took the blood chalice in his hand and offered it first to Licah.

"Bea, și a devenit unul."

As Licah sipped from the chalice with her left hand, Anca said, "Drink, and become one."

She passed the chalice to Saxton and he drank their blood.

Immediately when the blood passed their lips, their marks caught fire, and they each hit their knees in the dirt.

Wind kicked up on the plateau, causing each woman's hair to fly around wildly.

Geo grew nervous, him nearly yelling the last part of the rite.

"Licah Daciana, esti acum si pentru totdeauna Licah Lyall. Ai băut sânge de sotul tau, si nici o legătură este mai puternică decât cea a sângelui. Saxton Lyall, ia-ți nevasta in bratele tale si nu lasa sa plece."

Anca screamed the translation, having trouble staying on her feet.

"Licah Daciana, you are now and forever Licah Lyall. You just drank the blood of your husband, and no bond is stronger than that of blood. Saxton Lyall, take your wife into your arms and never let her go."

Just as Saxton reached for Licah, a black wolf bounded up the side of the plateau.

Saxton pulled Licah to his chest and took her lips with his own and time seemed to stand still.

Willard, in his wolf form, had pounced toward the group, but suddenly stopped, frozen in midair.

A blue tendril of light wove its way around his lupus body, and his fur began to dissipate.

Lila, who was sitting on the ground, looked down at her chest, saw a red tendril emanate from her mark, and weave its way toward Willard, who was only three feet away from his love.

Saxton and Licah held onto each other for dear life, watching as the same tendrils emanated from their own chests, and once those tendrils met, they gasped as they turned purple in color and exploded into a bright white light.

Lila and Willard's tendrils met and did the same, turning purple and exploding in a brilliance that left everyone with stars in their eyes.

Geo turned to Anca and gasped.

The woman was bathed from head to toe in red tendrils, and she wept silently.

"He's not here. He's gone," she said to Geo.

"What do I do?" she pleaded with him.

Geo was at a loss for words for the first time in his long life.

He opened his mouth to apologize, and then the racing wind kicked up even faster. A blue tendril climbed over the edge of the plateau.

They all watched in fascination as the tendril approached Anca and seemed to spin into a small cyclone until all the wind stopped, and what was left was the glowing blue image of a man.

Licah gasped, "Papa?"

Robert O'Riley smiled at his daughter, and then turned to his life mate.

"Anca, my love. I thought I would never see you again."

Anca, who was still bathed in red light, wept and said, "Robert, I miss you so."

"I'm sorry I ever left you that day. I'm sorry I can't be with you now. But I would like to marry you. I would like to be your husband before I have to go back."

Anca stood and approached the blue ghost of her late husband.

"Robert, you were and always will be, my one and only."

Robert stepped toward Anca and embraced her.

Their tendrils converged and turned brilliant purple as their lips met for the last time.

A white light exploded again, this time more brilliant than before, and they were each thrown backward by the force of it.

Anca lay on the ground with a smile on her face.

Robert was gone, but she felt him inside her, his love bathing her heart.

Saxton reached for Licah, their hands still bound by the silken cloth, now stained red with their combined blood.

Licah looked for her grandmother and found her wrapped around Willard, who was as naked as the day he was born.

"I can't believe it. It worked," Saxton whispered to his wife.

Licah looked into his eyes and reached for the amulet.

Saxton grabbed her hand.

"Are you sure?" he asked, still concerned for her safety, even though the proof was before him.

Licah nodded and pulled the amulet over his head.

Once it left his neck, it disintegrated in her hand and fell to the ground, dust.

Epilogue

Licah and Saxton sat in their newly built home in Parker's Ridge watching Anca, Willard, and Lila decorate the Christmas Tree.

Licah's newest novel, *Fear the Beast Within*, lay on the coffee table next to two bottles of water and some prenatal vitamins.

"No, it doesn't go that way, Dad, it goes around the tree," Anca scolded, grabbing the string of golden beads from his hands.

Willard smiled at his daughter and handed them over.

Refusing to be apart any longer, they had all moved in together.

Now, with little Robert Lyall on the way, they had even more reason to stay a tight knit family.

Saxton kissed the top of Licah's head and placed his hand on her stomach, which was only starting to round out.

He couldn't wait to meet their son.

"I love you," he said, looking into her eyes.

"I love you," she replied, kissing his lips ever so softly.

"Now, don't you be starting that again," Willard scolded, "Last night, you kept Lila and me up all night with your moaning and such."

They both turned, looking at the great-grandfather-to-be in shock. Licah blushed and Saxton laughed.

"Watch it, old man, I can think of a few nights where we heard the same."

The doorbell rang and Saxton left his beloved wife to open the door. Geo stood on the front steps, so many presents in his arms that you could barely see the top of his head.

Saxton grabbed a few to help the old man and smiled at the weight of them.

"What did you bring, Geo?"

Geo smiled and cocked his head to the side.

"Books, what do you think?"

Acknowledgements
by L R Barrett-Durham

I would like to thank E G Glover for all his hard work and dedication to this book. We wrote this novel in thirty-seven days, and I've never in my life been more in tune with someone on something like this.

I would also like to thank JoAnna Pennington, who read this novel while E G and I were writing it. Her opinions and observations were paramount to the completion of this book. She's always read anything and everything I've ever written and is amazing at giving me feedback. Girl, you are definitely our number one fan.

I would like to thank the Ladies of the Round Table of Listerhill Credit Union. You ladies are amazing.

I would like to thank all my friends and family for their support in all my endeavors, whether it is writing, stained glass, or music. I couldn't do it without you.

Also, I would like to thank James and Patrick for putting up with all the time I spend writing and putting things aside.

Lastly, but most importantly, I would like to thank God, who holds me in his hands every day and never, ever gives up on me.

Acknowledgements
by E G Glover

I would like to thank everyone that has shown a genuine interest in this book, of which there are too many to call by name. However, I would like to start by thanking my co-author and friend L R Barrett-Durham, who showed me how to have faith in my writing ability.

I also have to mention my daughter, Annika, who is one of the bravest people I know. You have taught me to be a stronger person.

To Anne, who said this book has been in me for over a decade.

I cannot forget to mention JoAnna Pennington, our number one fan. She eats up anything I put into print.

To Sasha, my inspiration for the character of Licah and an amazing child nurse practitioner at Children's Hospital.

I would like to thank Karina Coleman and Connie McGuire for helping with my end of the editing. It's not the first time Mrs. McGuire has 'graded' my work.

Finally, the most important, I acknowledge God and his amazing power. He is the whole reason that my daughter is here today and that I am here to write this book.

Stay Tuned for

Fear the

Thirst Within

Book Two: The Fear Series

(Winter 2012)

By L R Barrett-Durham
and E G Glover

Check out these books by
L R Barrett-Durham

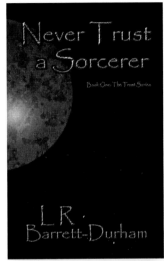

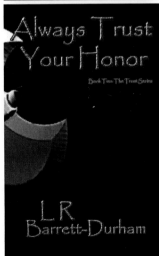

About the Authors:

Photo by JoAnna Pennington

L R Barrett-Durham

(Written by E G Glover)

L R Barrett-Durham is one of the most talented people I have ever met. There is no obstacle she cannot overcome. Her ability to tap into her creative abilities is a feat I have never seen in real life, until now. She is a true Renaissance Lady and has more patience and understanding than anyone I've ever met. She is a great friend to yours truly and has shown me how to unlock my writing potential. We have a writing partnership that I see continuing for years to come.

She lives with her family in Cherokee, AL. She is employed as a Network Technician, but her true loves are various types of artwork, music, writing and being a mother.

E G Glover

(Written by L R Barrett-Durham)

I've never met a braver soul than E G Glover. His strength and courage are incredible. He has overcome so many hardships in his life and has not let them get him down. He is an amazing, talented writer and an even more amazing friend. Thank you for everything E G. You are the man.

E G Glover lives in Killen, Alabama, with his family. He enjoys all things nerdy (L R's word) and is a Doctor Who fanatic.